#2 NEVER MAKE A GIANT MAD

Artur Laperla

Graphic Universe™ • Minneapolis

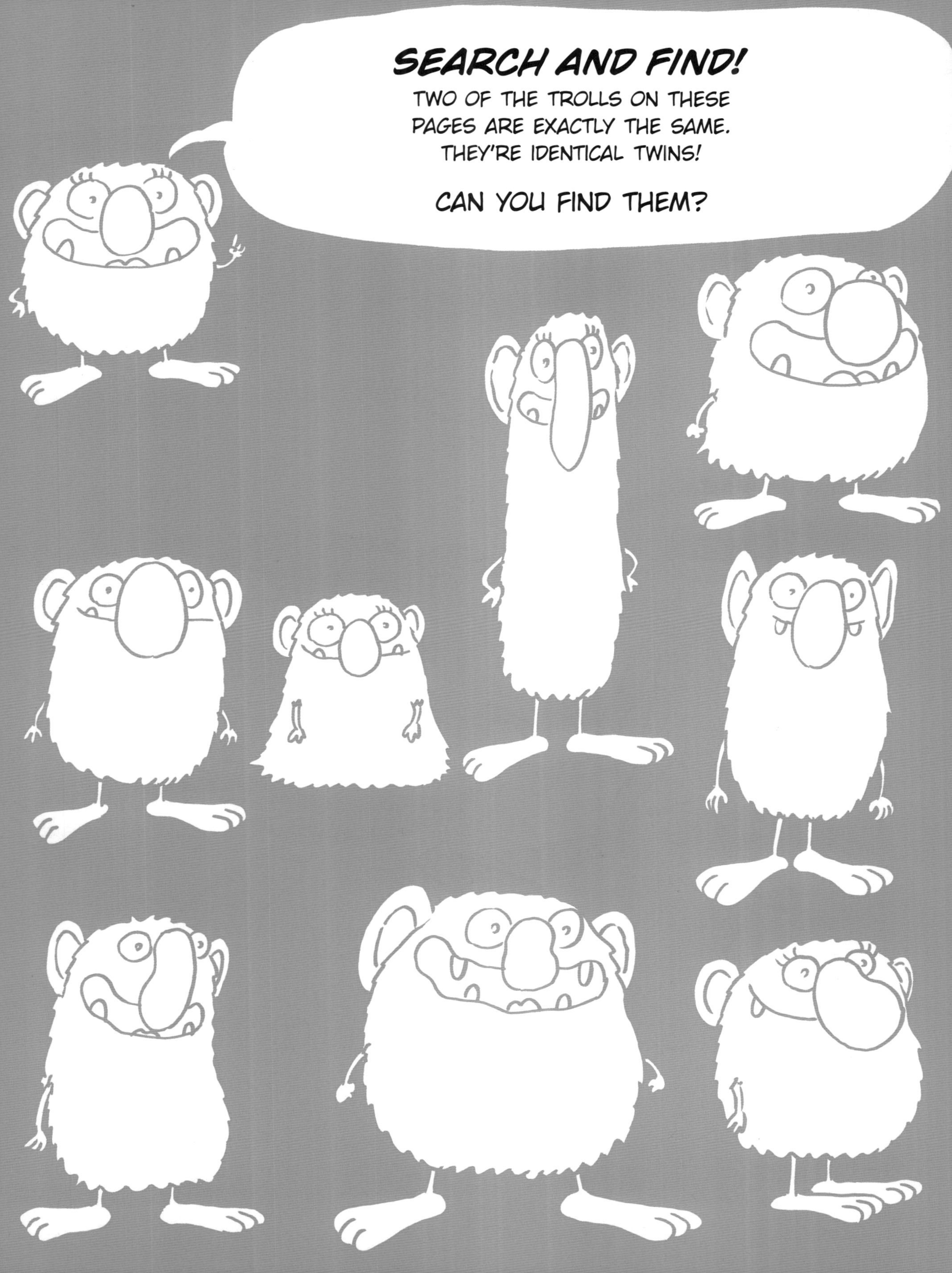
SEARCH AND FIND!
TWO OF THE TROLLS ON THESE PAGES ARE EXACTLY THE SAME. THEY'RE IDENTICAL TWINS!
CAN YOU FIND THEM?

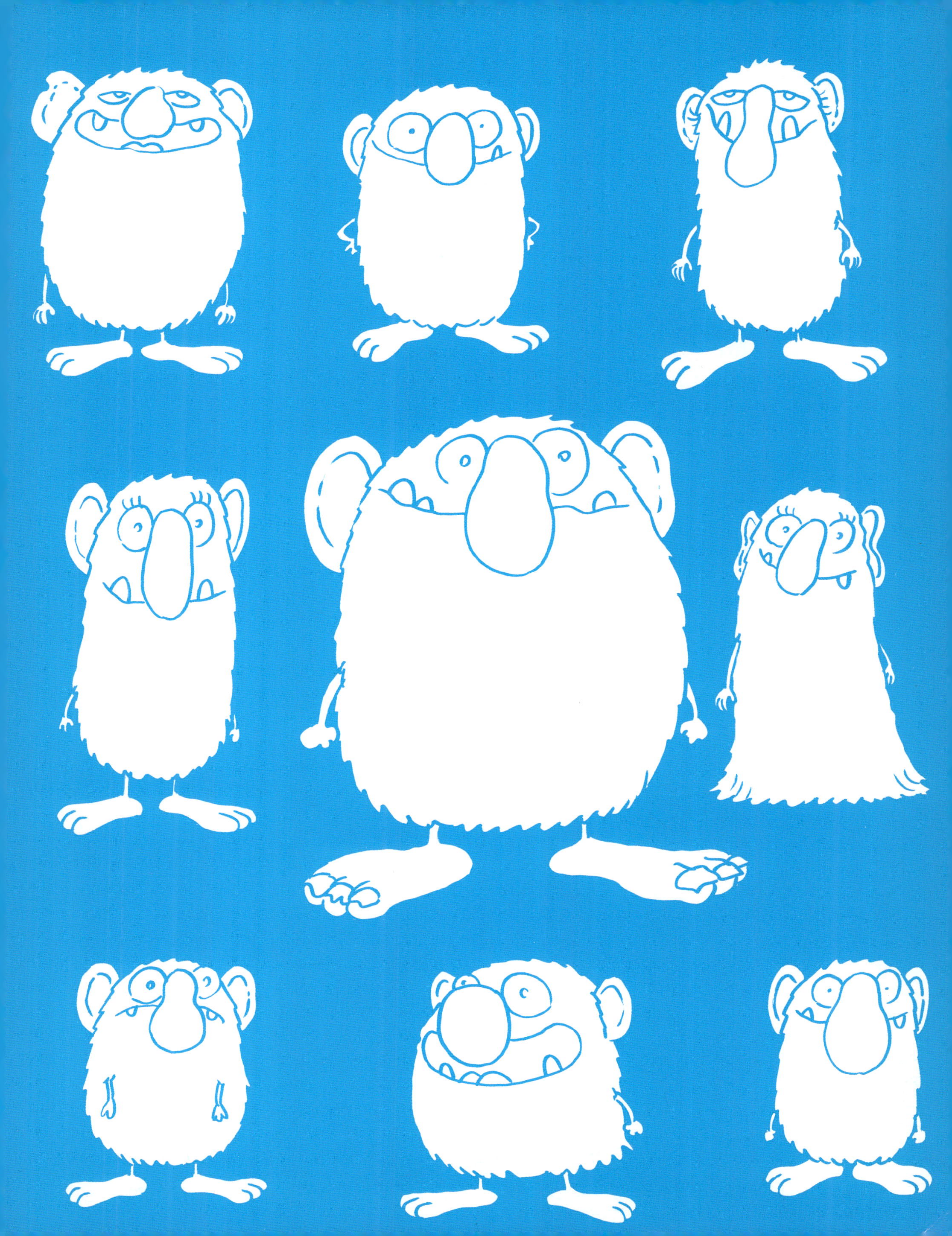

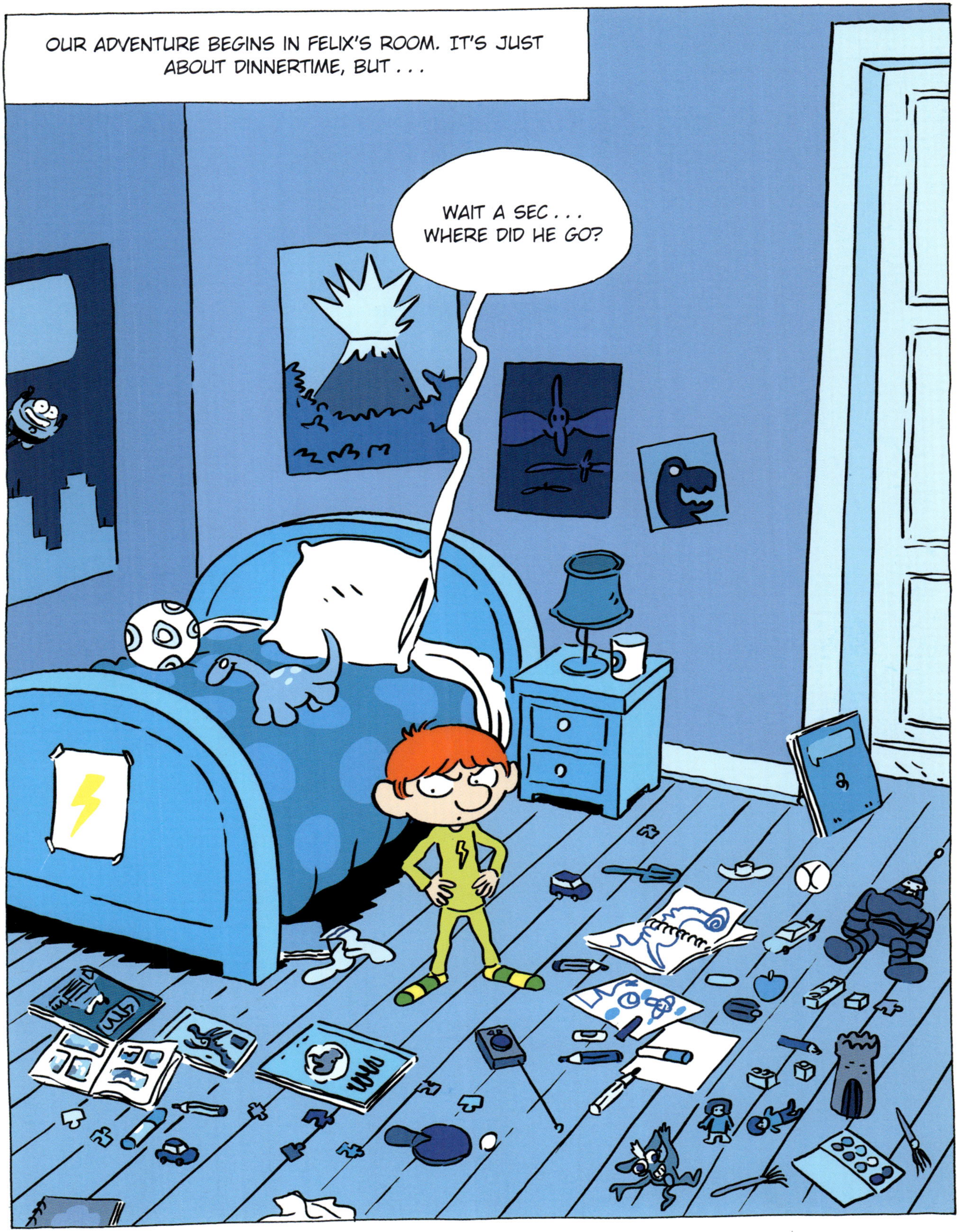
OUR ADVENTURE BEGINS IN FELIX'S ROOM. IT'S JUST ABOUT DINNERTIME, BUT . . .
WAIT A SEC . . . WHERE DID HE GO?

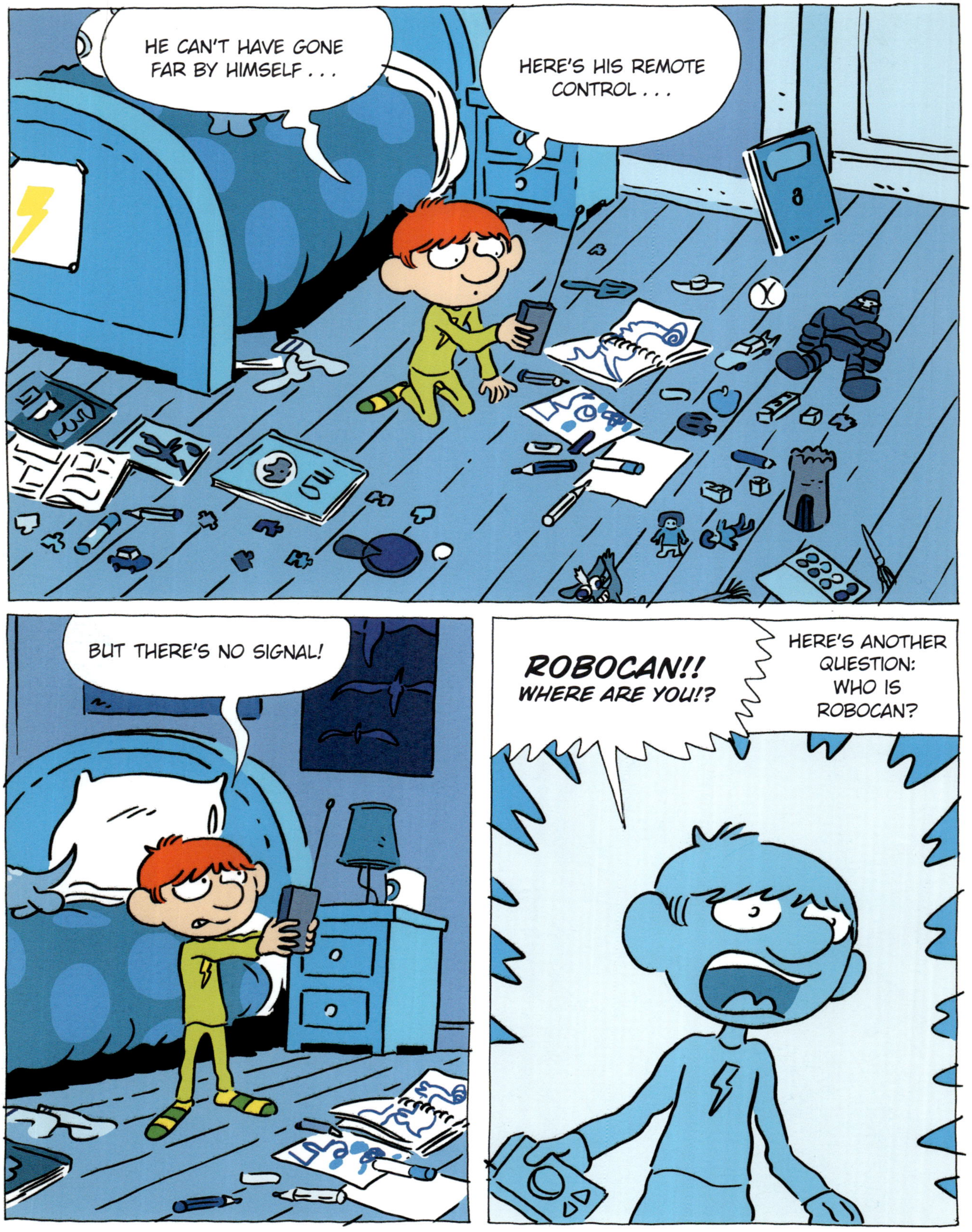
HE CAN'T HAVE GONE FAR BY HIMSELF . . .
HERE'S HIS REMOTE CONTROL . . .
BUT THERE'S NO SIGNAL!
ROBOCAN!! WHERE ARE YOU!?
HERE'S ANOTHER QUESTION: WHO IS ROBOCAN?

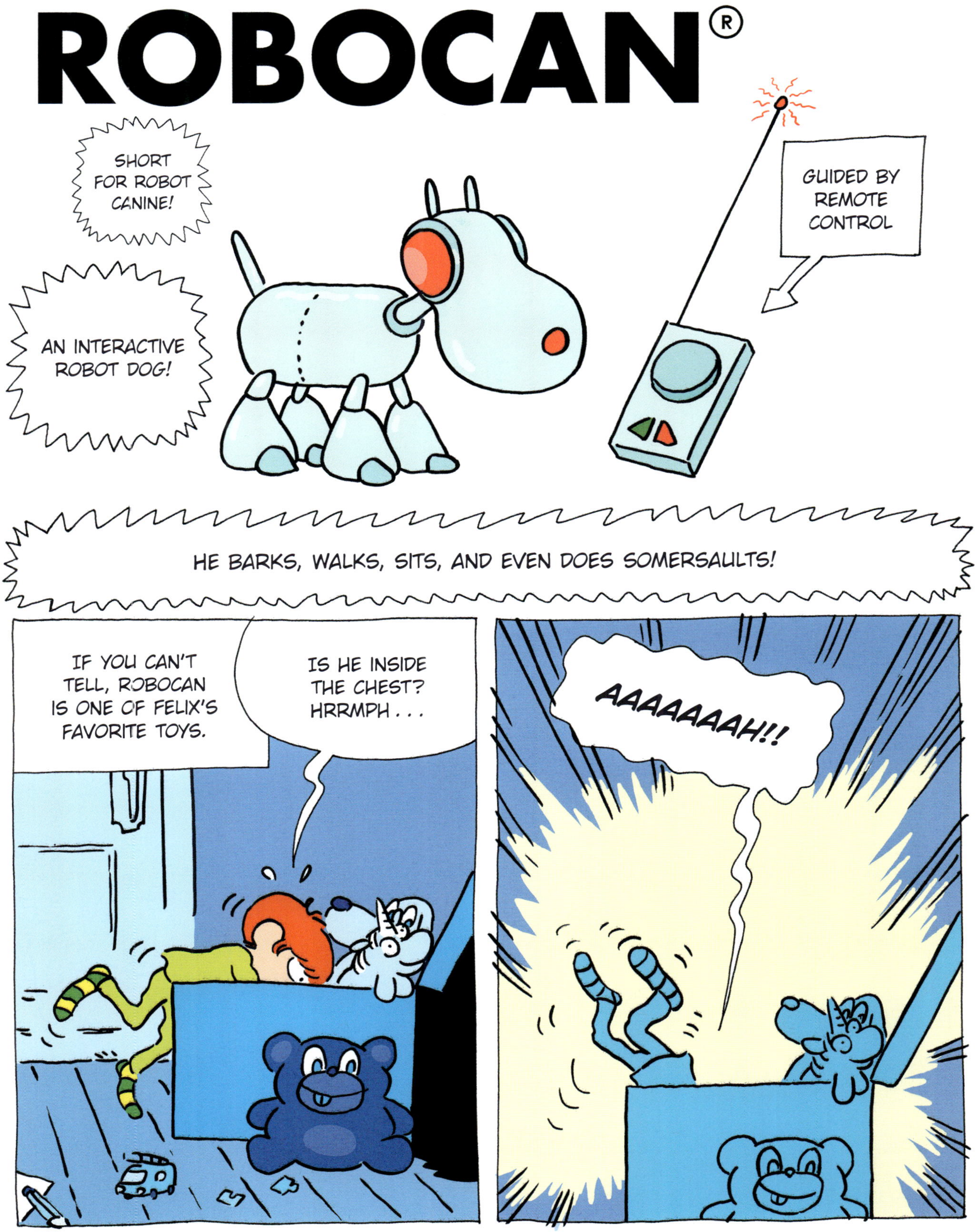
ROBOCAN®
SHORT FOR ROBOT CANINE!
AN INTERACTIVE ROBOT DOG!
GUIDED BY REMOTE CONTROL
HE BARKS, WALKS, SITS, AND EVEN DOES SOMERSAULTS!
IF YOU CAN'T TELL, ROBOCAN IS ONE OF FELIX'S FAVORITE TOYS.
IS HE INSIDE THE CHEST? HRRMPH . . .
AAAAAAAAH!!

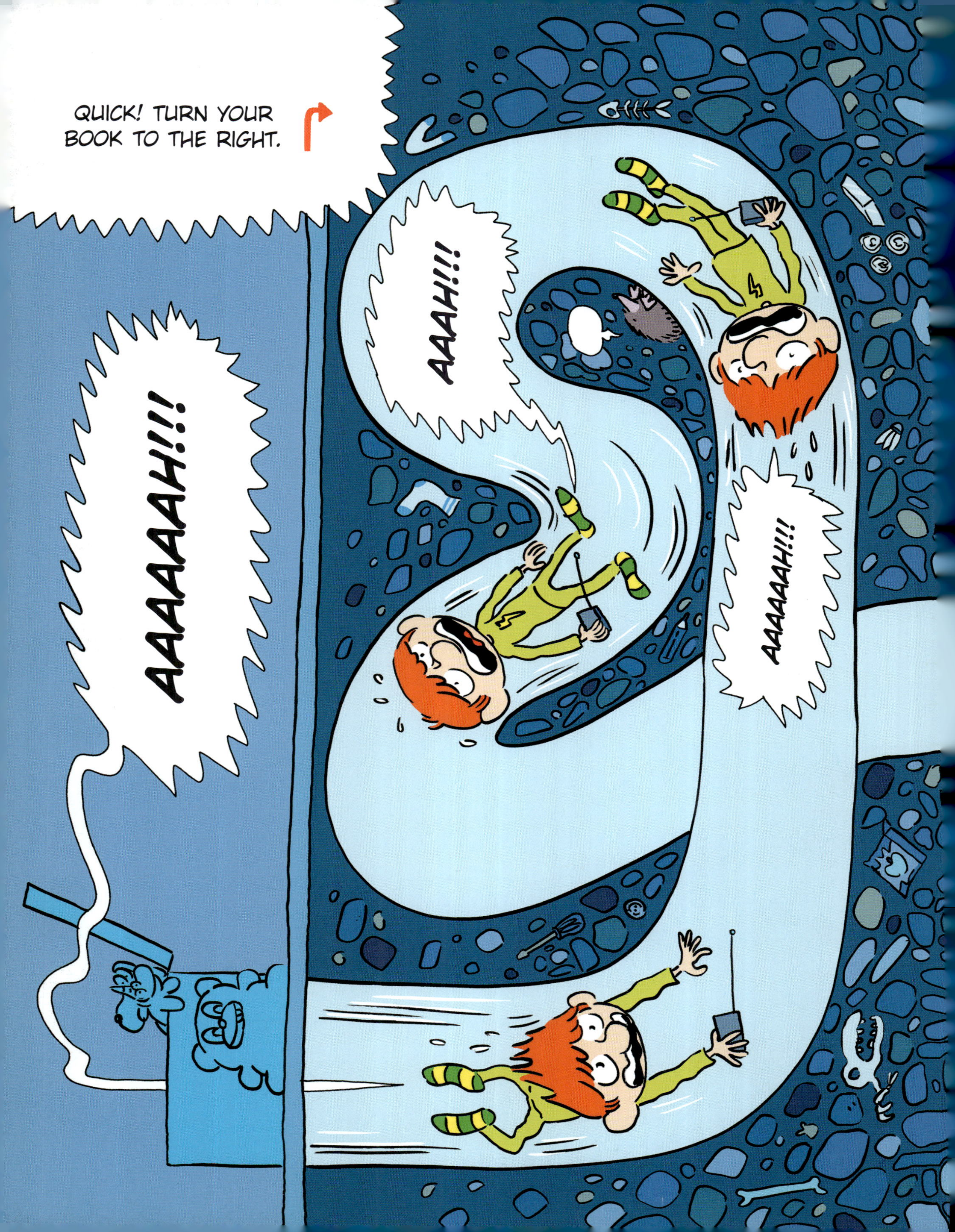
QUICK! TURN YOUR BOOK TO THE RIGHT.
AAAAAAH!!!
AAAH!!!
AAAAAH!!!

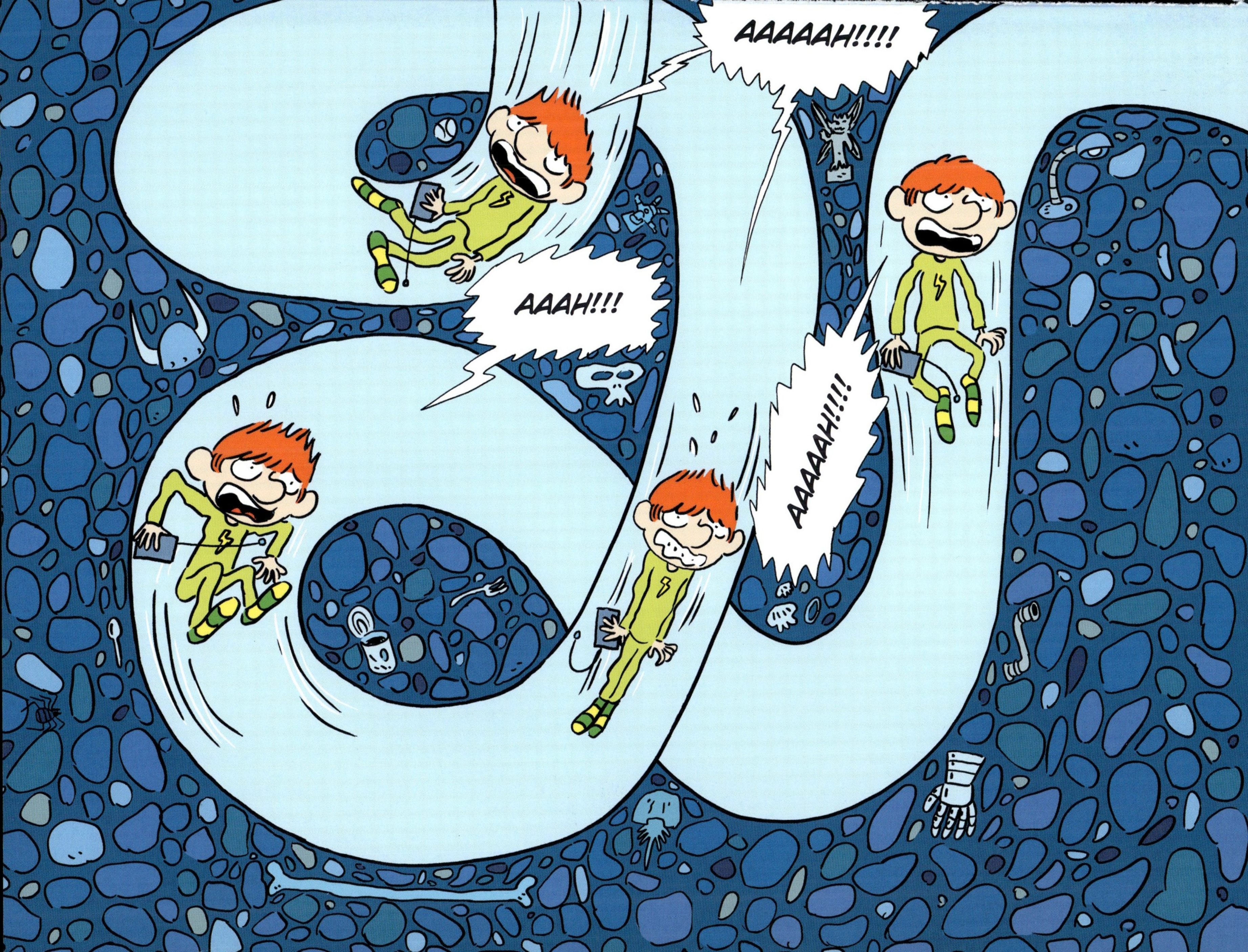
AAAAAH!!!!
AAAH!!!
AAAAAH!!!!

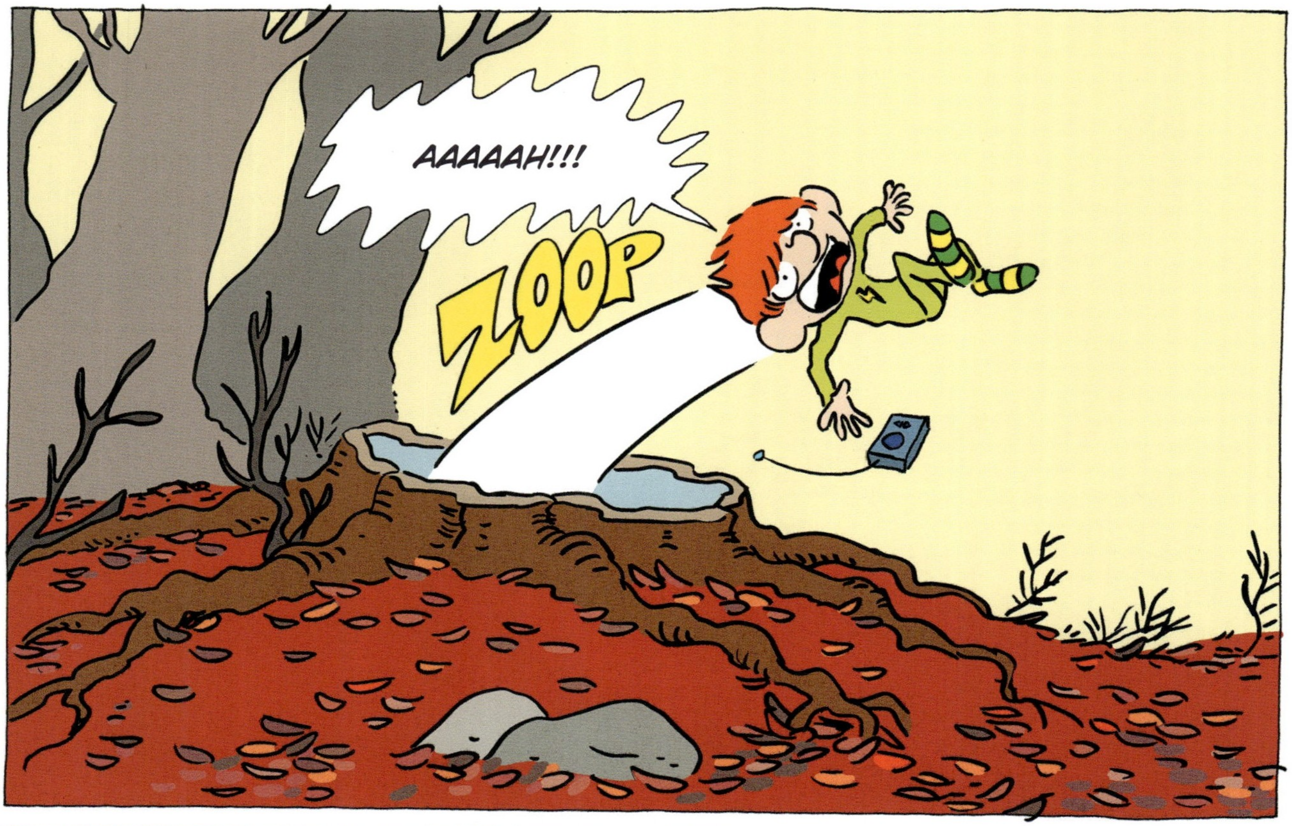
AAAAAH!!!
ZOOP

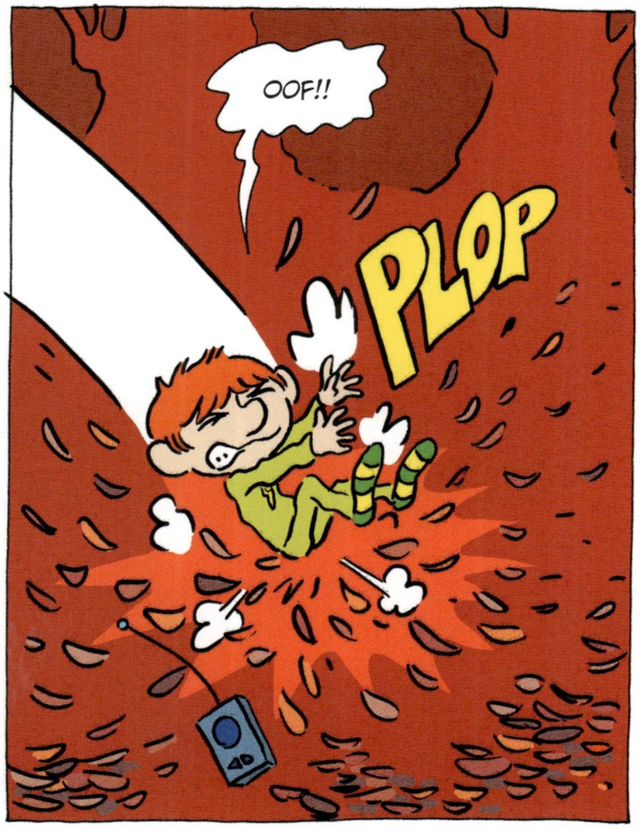
OOF!!
PLOP

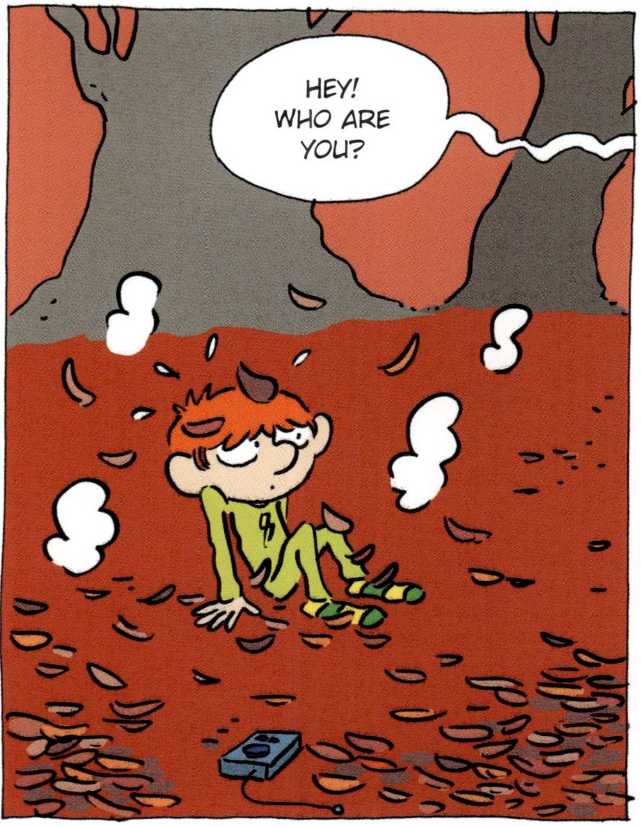
HEY!
WHO ARE
YOU?

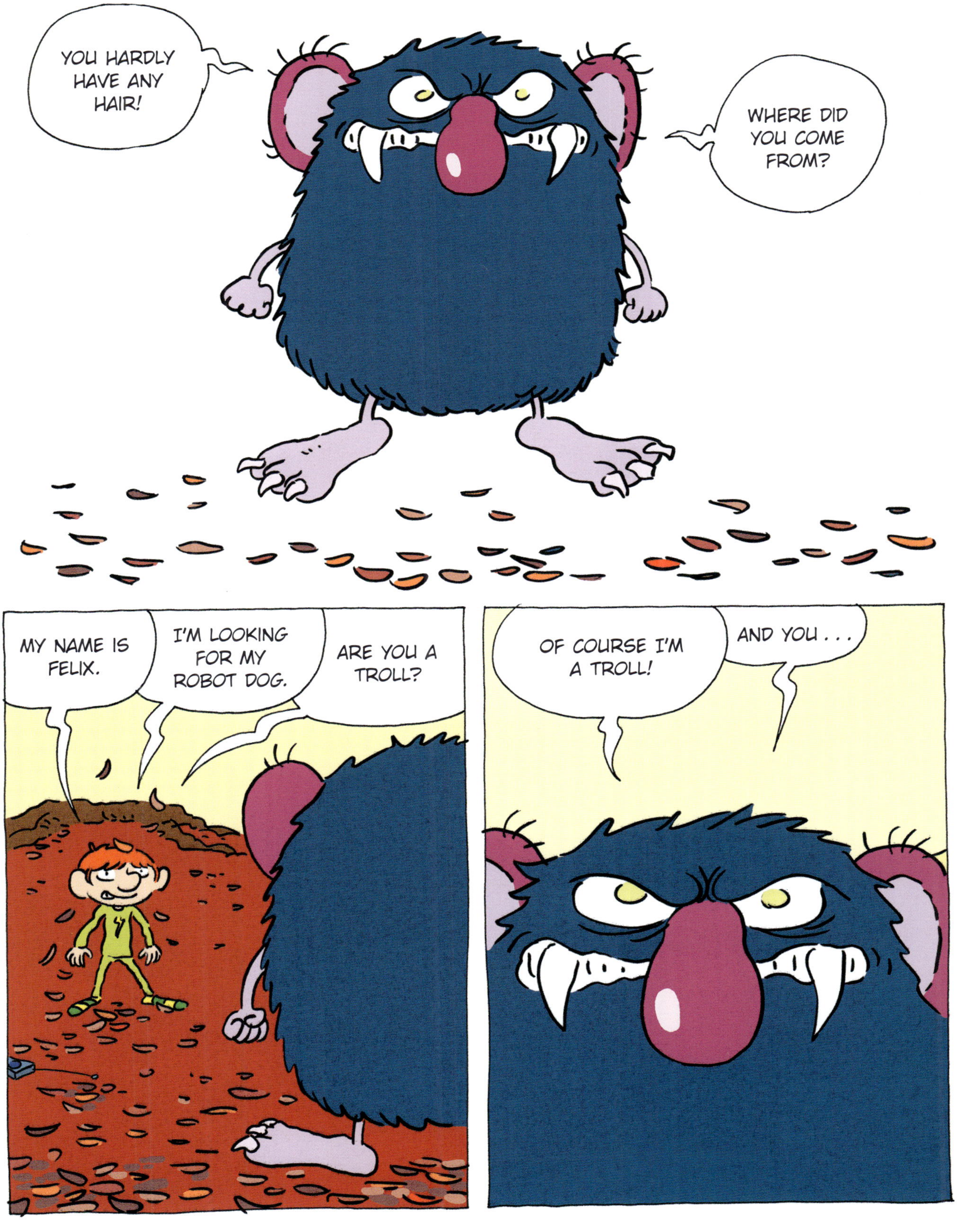
YOU HARDLY HAVE ANY HAIR!
WHERE DID YOU COME FROM?
MY NAME IS FELIX.
I'M LOOKING FOR MY ROBOT DOG.
ARE YOU A TROLL?
OF COURSE I'M A TROLL!
AND YOU . . .

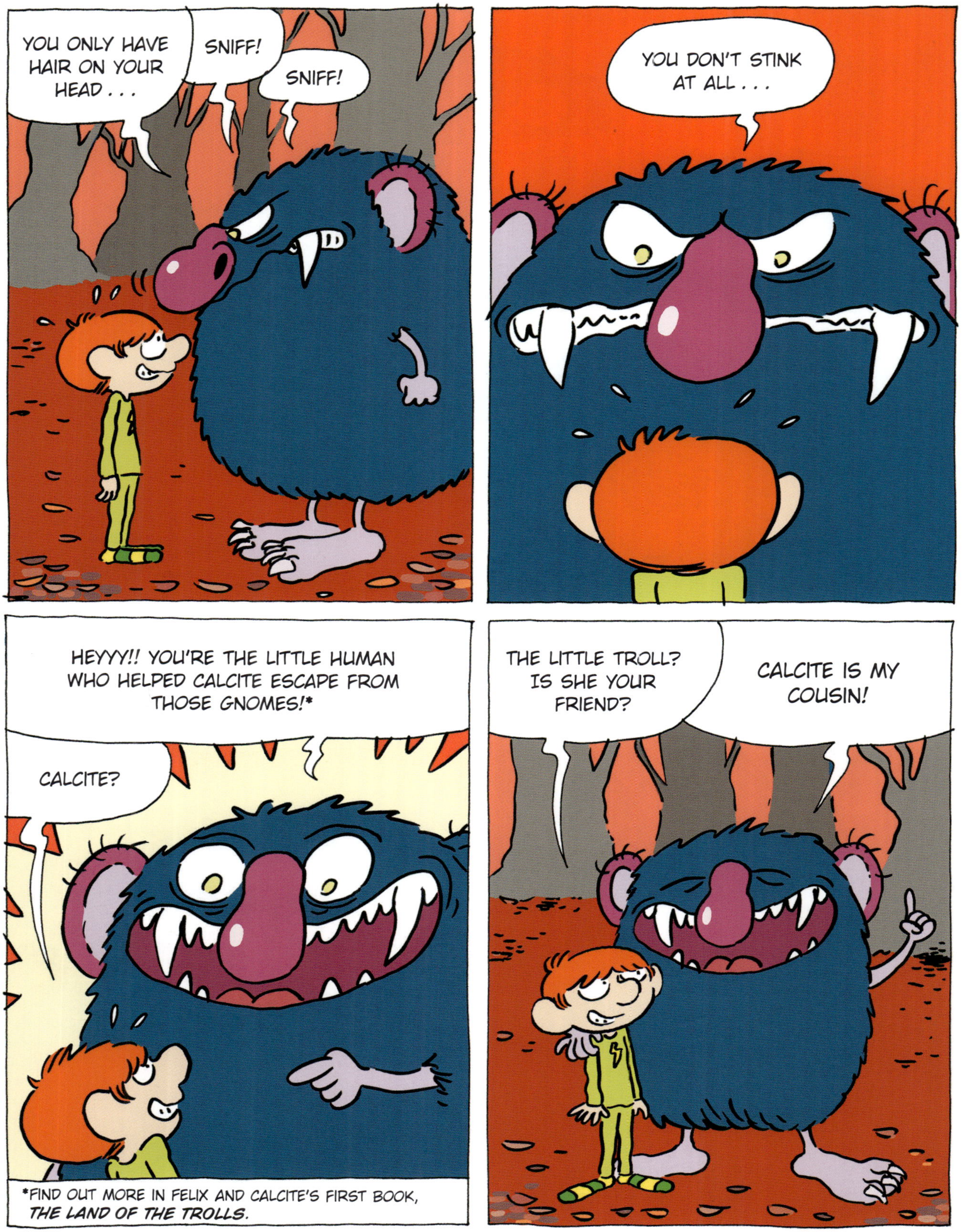
YOU ONLY HAVE HAIR ON YOUR HEAD . . .
SNIFF!
SNIFF!
YOU DON'T STINK AT ALL . . .
HEYYY!! YOU'RE THE LITTLE HUMAN WHO HELPED CALCITE ESCAPE FROM THOSE GNOMES!*
CALCITE?
THE LITTLE TROLL? IS SHE YOUR FRIEND?
CALCITE IS MY COUSIN!
*FIND OUT MORE IN FELIX AND CALCITE'S FIRST BOOK, ***THE LAND OF THE TROLLS.***

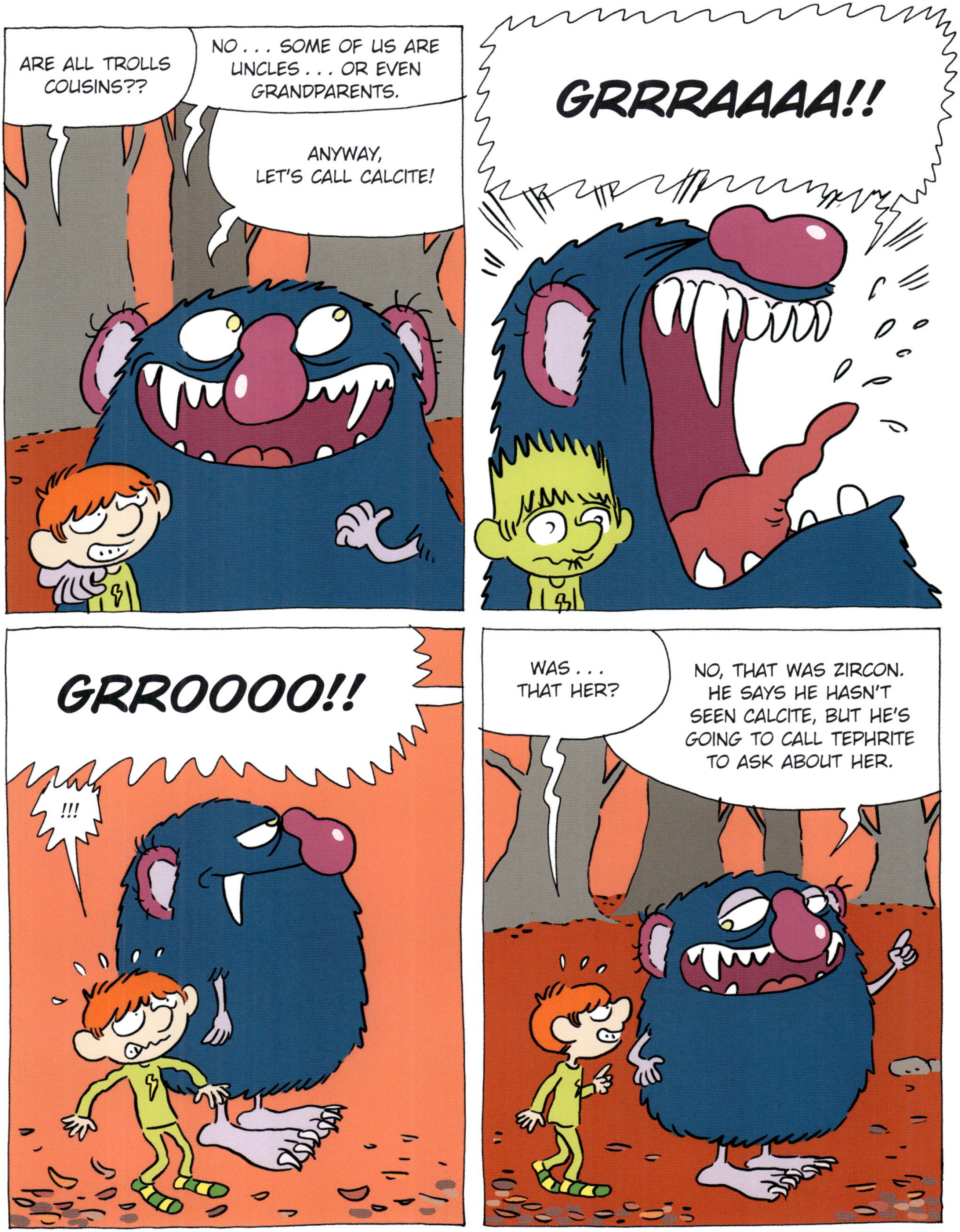
ARE ALL TROLLS COUSINS??
NO . . . SOME OF US ARE UNCLES . . . OR EVEN GRANDPARENTS.
ANYWAY, LET'S CALL CALCITE!
GRRRAAAA!!
GRROOOO!!
!!!
WAS . . . THAT HER?
NO, THAT WAS ZIRCON. HE SAYS HE HASN'T SEEN CALCITE, BUT HE'S GOING TO CALL TEPHRITE TO ASK ABOUT HER.

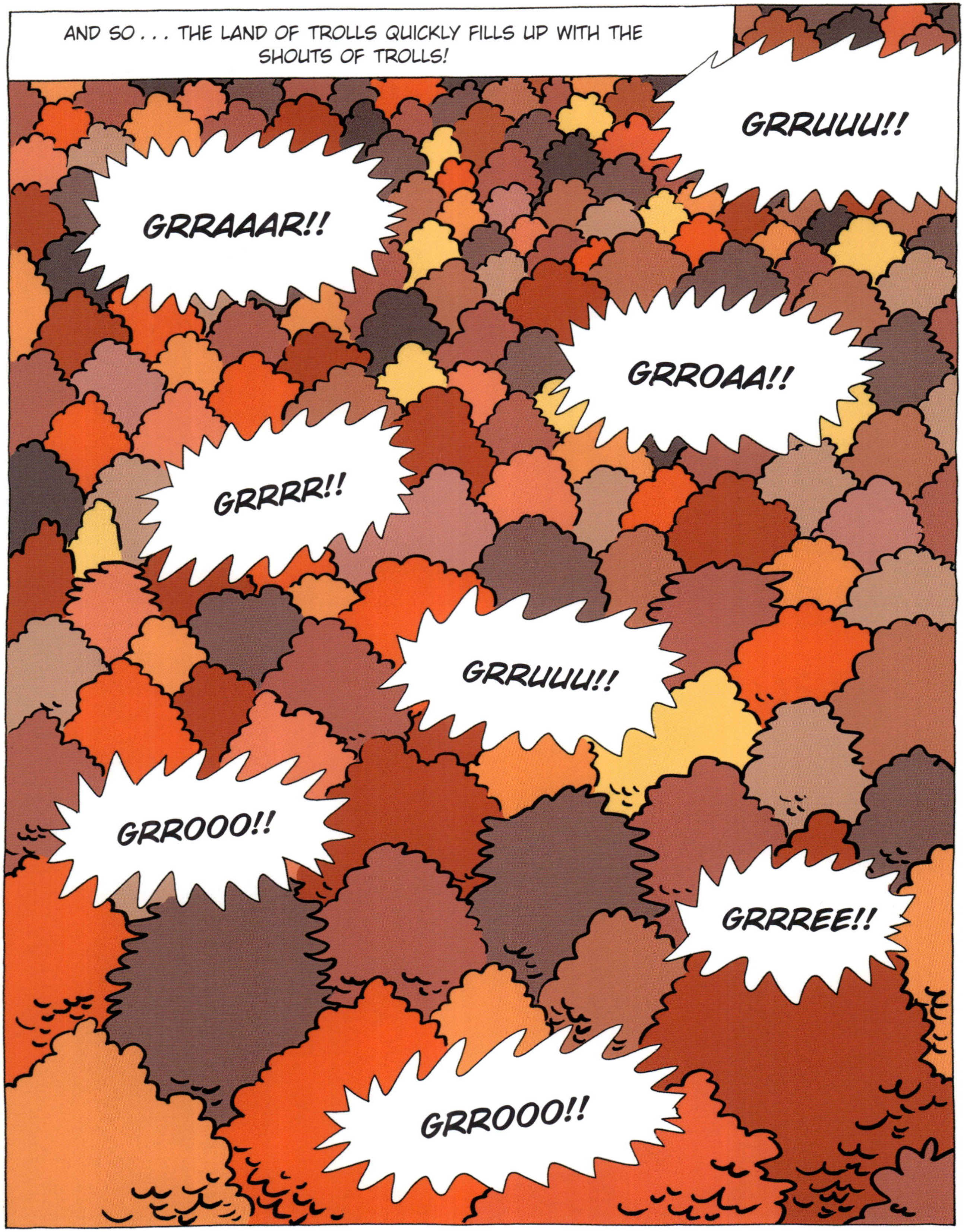
AND SO . . . THE LAND OF TROLLS QUICKLY FILLS UP WITH THE SHOUTS OF TROLLS!
GRRAAAR!!
GRRUUU!!
GRROAA!!
GRRRR!!
GRRUUU!!
GRROOO!!
GRRREE!!
GRROOO!!

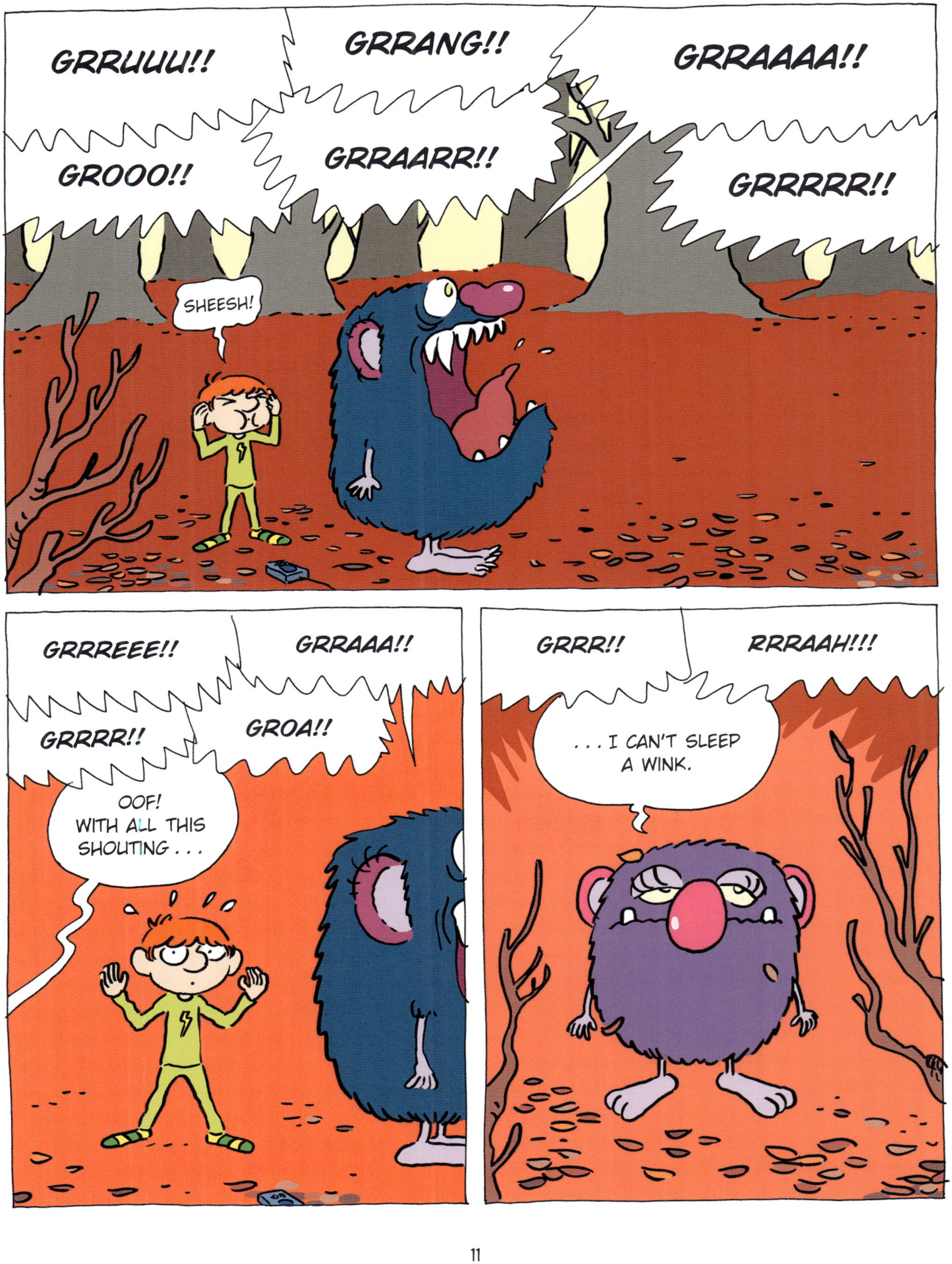
GRRUUU!!
GRRANG!!
GRRAAAA!!
GROOO!!
GRRAARR!!
GRRRRR!!
SHEESH!
GRRREEE!!
GRRAAA!!
GRRRR!!
GROA!!
OOF! WITH ALL THIS SHOUTING . . .
GRRR!!
RRRAAH!!!
. . . I CAN'T SLEEP A WINK.

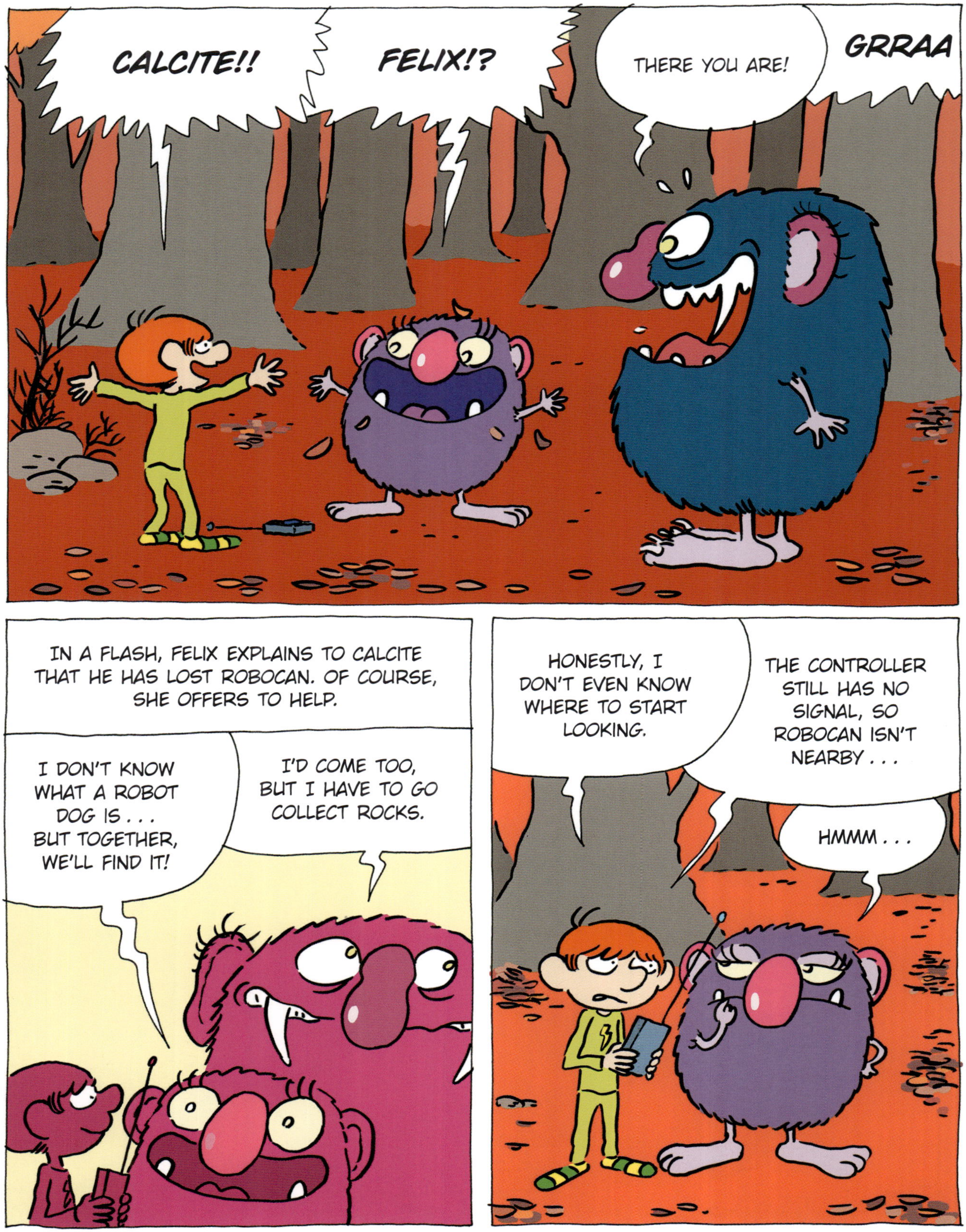
CALCITE!!
FELIX!?
THERE YOU ARE!
GRRAA
IN A FLASH, FELIX EXPLAINS TO CALCITE THAT HE HAS LOST ROBOCAN. OF COURSE, SHE OFFERS TO HELP.
I DON'T KNOW WHAT A ROBOT DOG IS . . . BUT TOGETHER, WE'LL FIND IT!
I'D COME TOO, BUT I HAVE TO GO COLLECT ROCKS.
HONESTLY, I DON'T EVEN KNOW WHERE TO START LOOKING.
THE CONTROLLER STILL HAS NO SIGNAL, SO ROBOCAN ISN'T NEARBY . . .
HMMM . . .

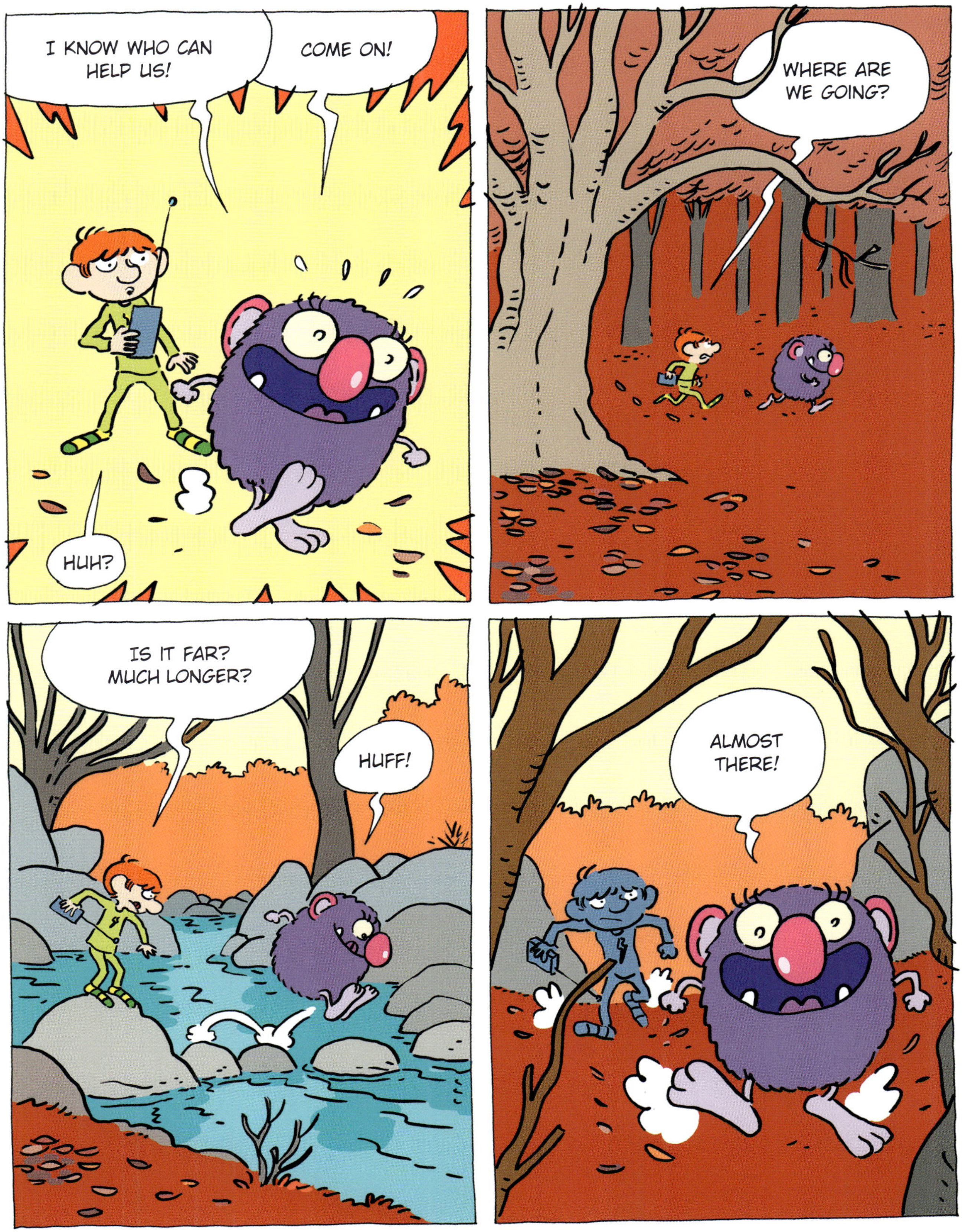
I KNOW WHO CAN HELP US!
COME ON!
HUH?
WHERE ARE WE GOING?
IS IT FAR? MUCH LONGER?
HUFF!
ALMOST THERE!

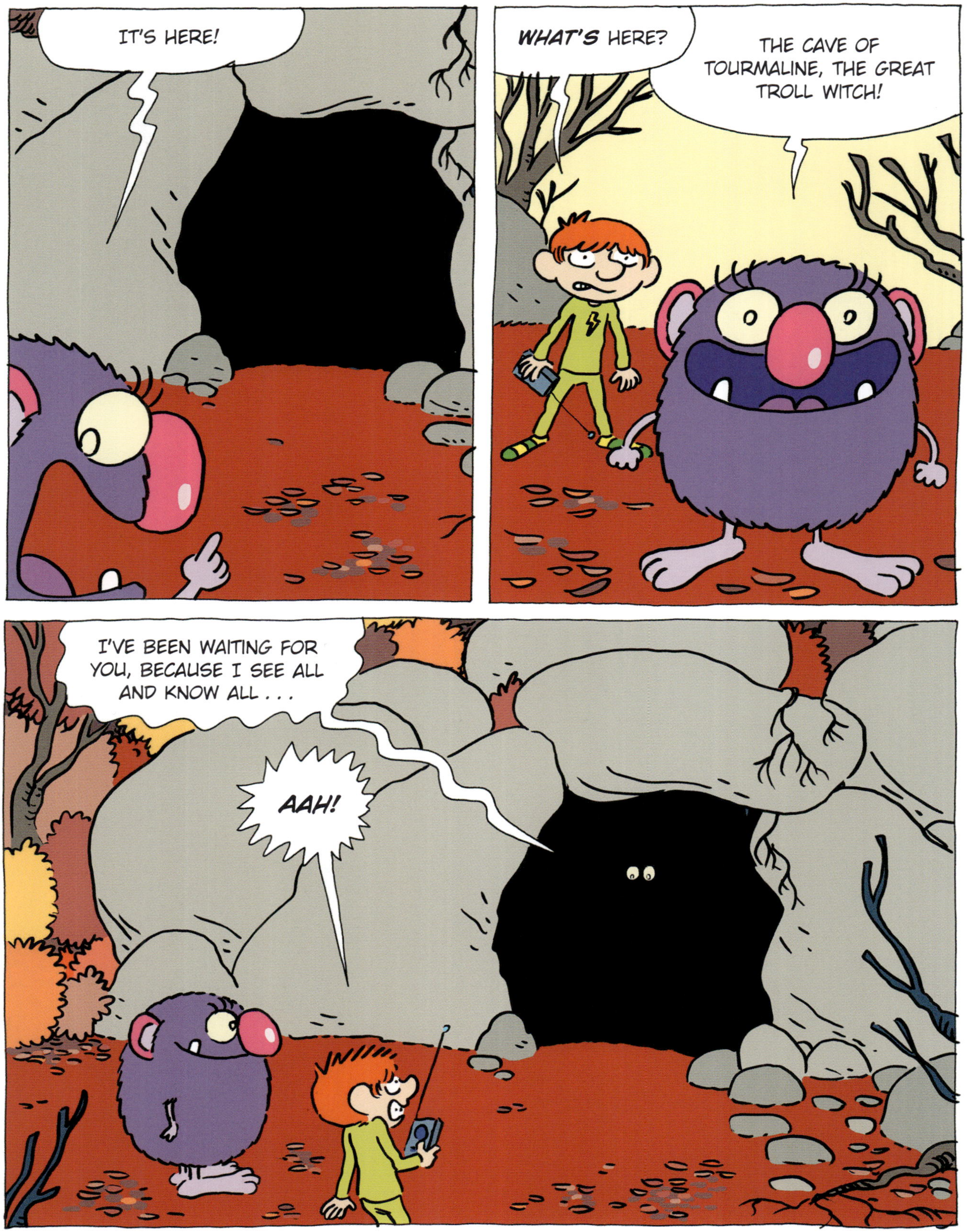
IT'S HERE!
WHAT'S HERE?
THE CAVE OF TOURMALINE, THE GREAT TROLL WITCH!
I'VE BEEN WAITING FOR YOU, BECAUSE I SEE ALL AND KNOW ALL . . .
AAH!

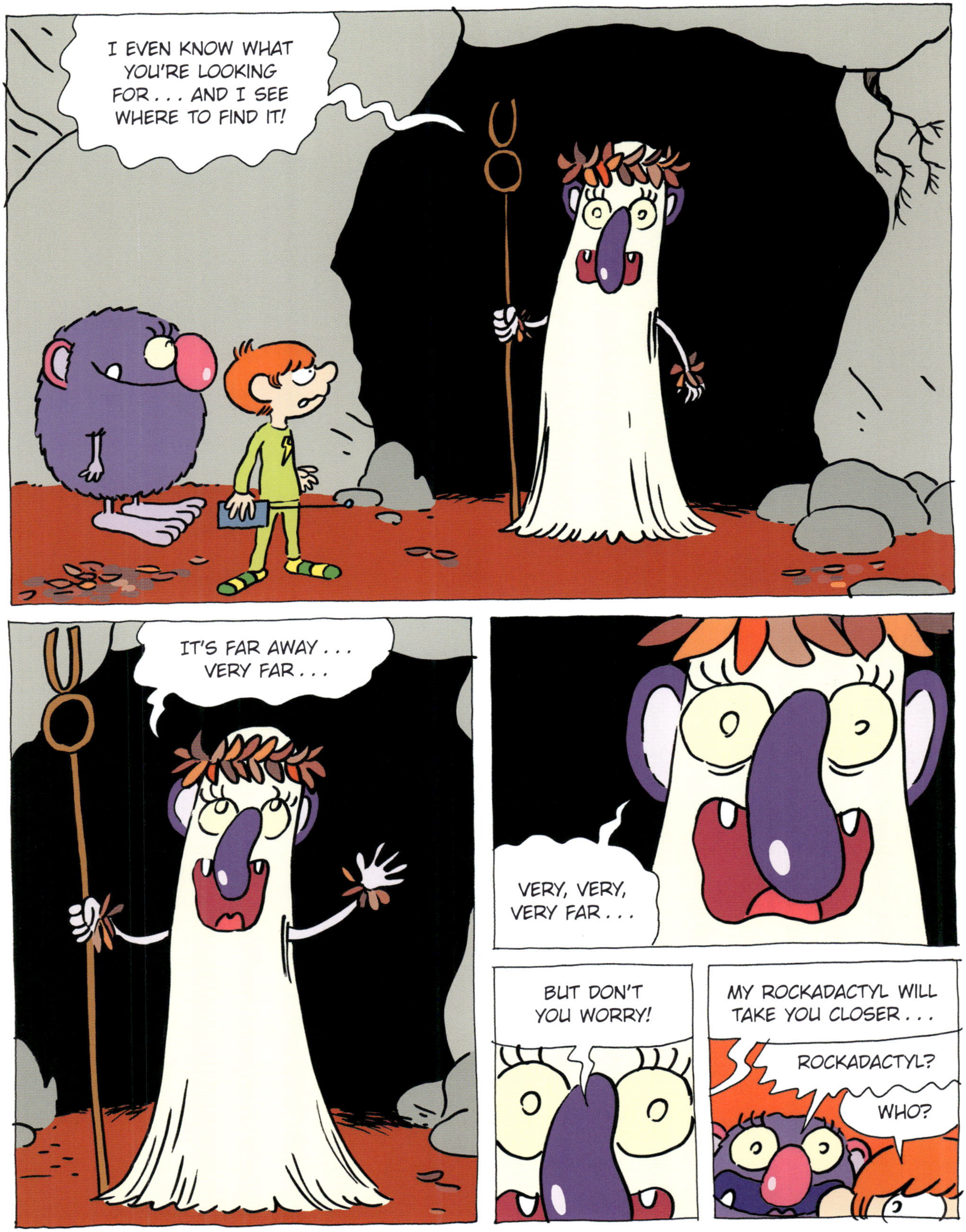
I EVEN KNOW WHAT YOU'RE LOOKING FOR . . . AND I SEE WHERE TO FIND IT!
IT'S FAR AWAY . . . VERY FAR . . .
VERY, VERY, VERY FAR . . .
BUT DON'T YOU WORRY!
MY ROCKADACTYL WILL TAKE YOU CLOSER . . .
ROCKADACTYL?
WHO?

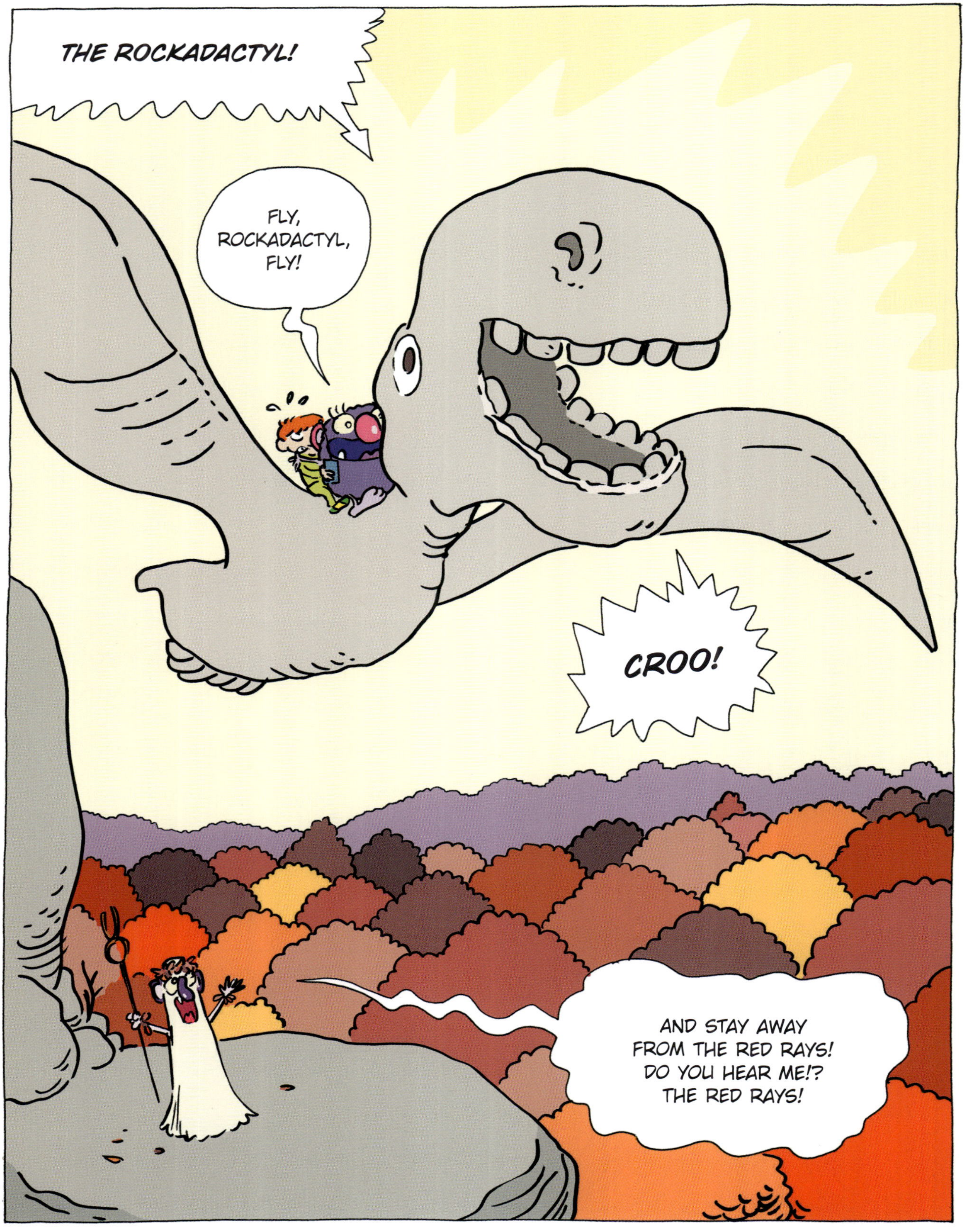
THE ROCKADACTYL!
FLY, ROCKADACTYL, FLY!
CROO!
AND STAY AWAY FROM THE RED RAYS! DO YOU HEAR ME!? THE RED RAYS!

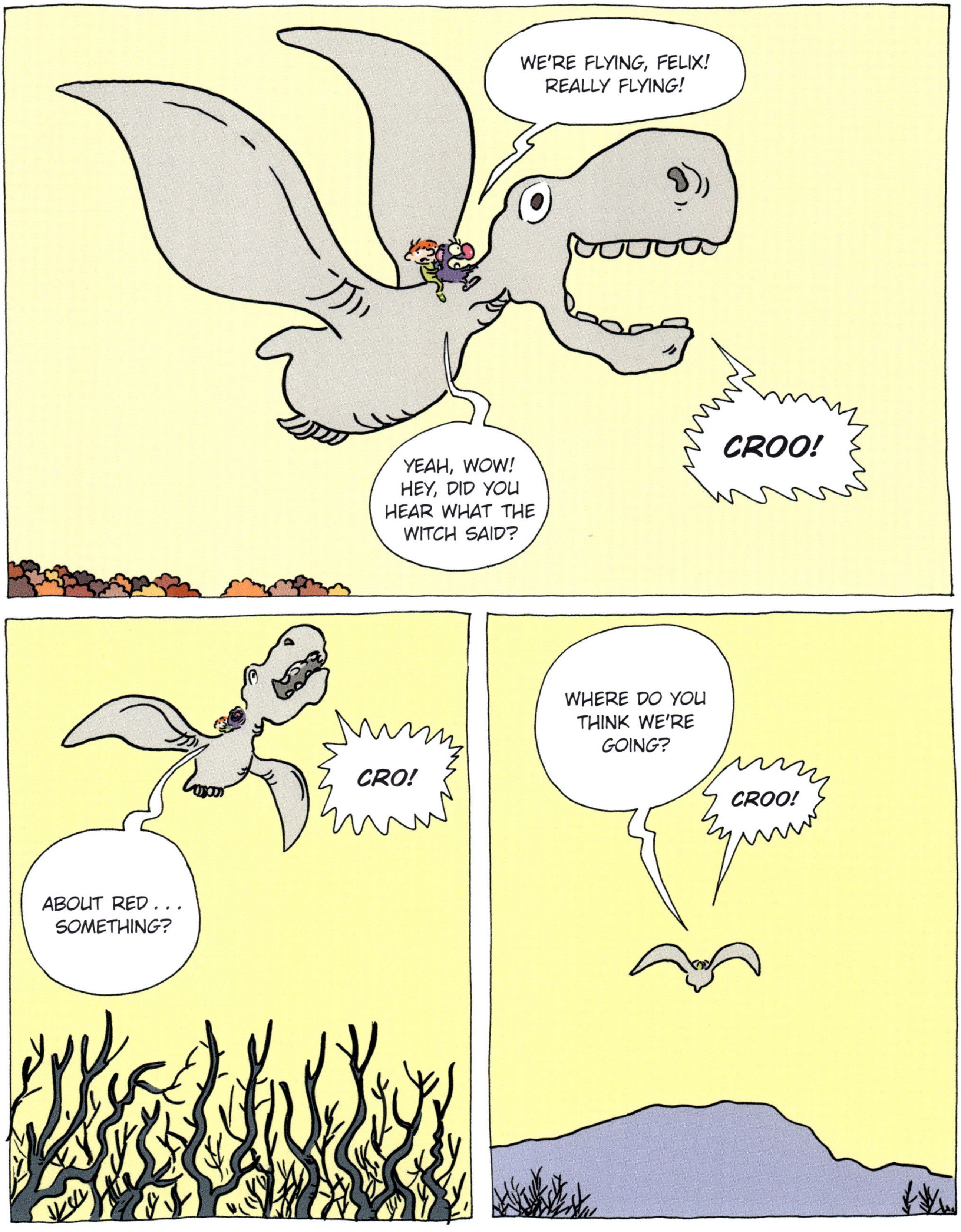
WE'RE FLYING, FELIX! REALLY FLYING!
YEAH, WOW! HEY, DID YOU HEAR WHAT THE WITCH SAID?
CROO!
CRO!
ABOUT RED . . . SOMETHING?
WHERE DO YOU THINK WE'RE GOING?
CROO!

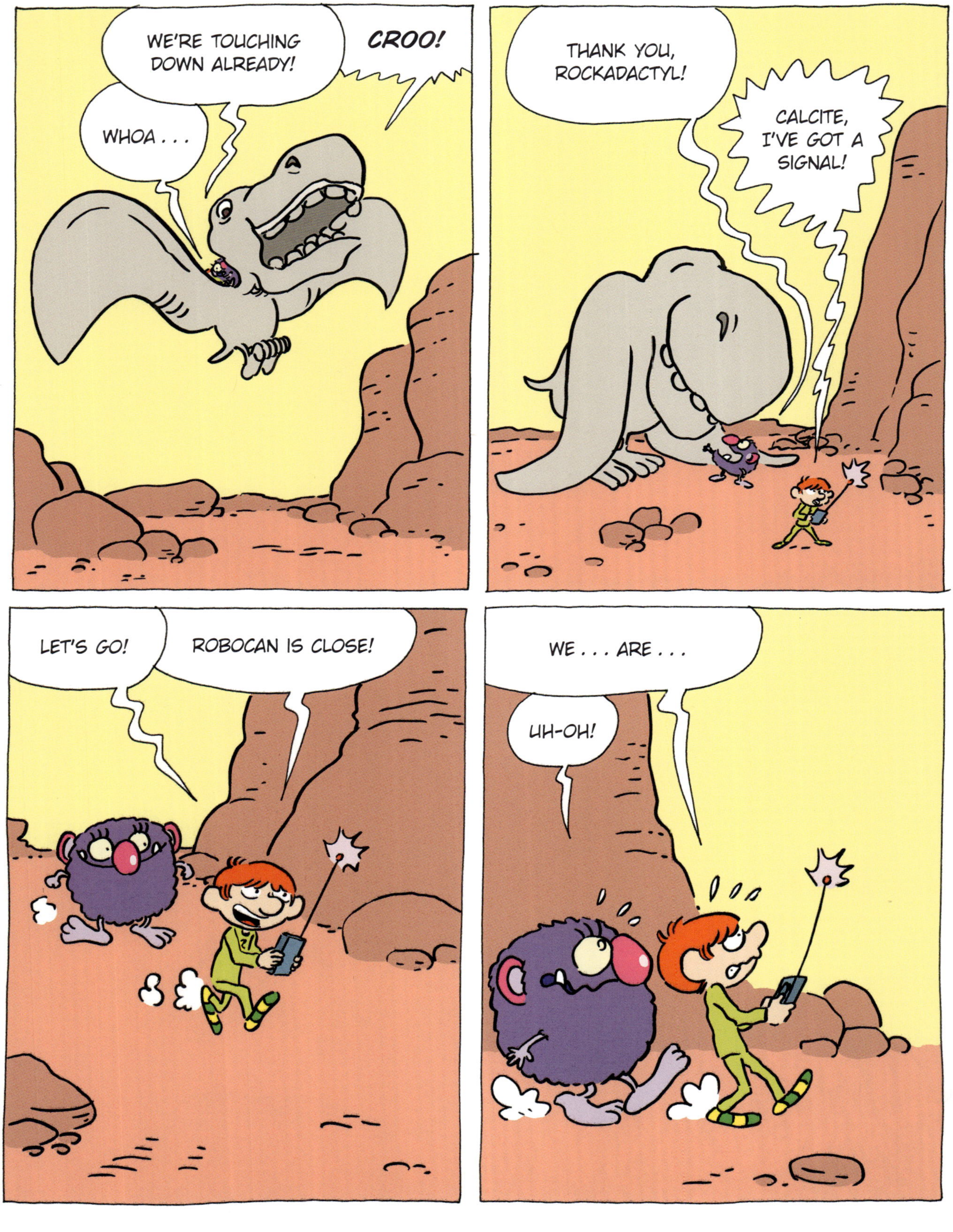
WHOA . . .
WE'RE TOUCHING DOWN ALREADY!
CROO!
THANK YOU, ROCKADACTYL!
CALCITE, I'VE GOT A SIGNAL!
LET'S GO!
ROBOCAN IS CLOSE!
WE . . . ARE . . .
UH-OH!

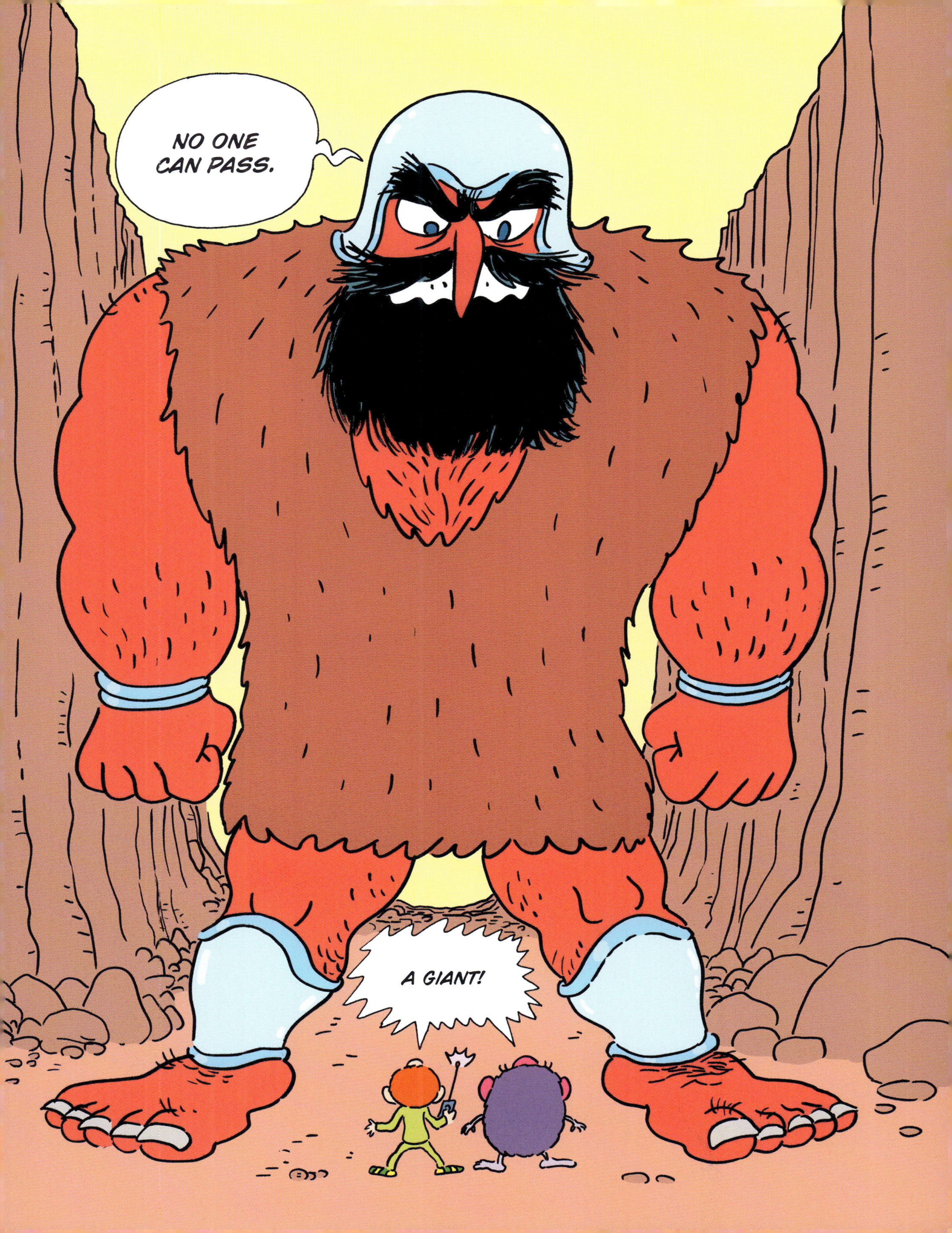
NO ONE CAN PASS.
A GIANT!

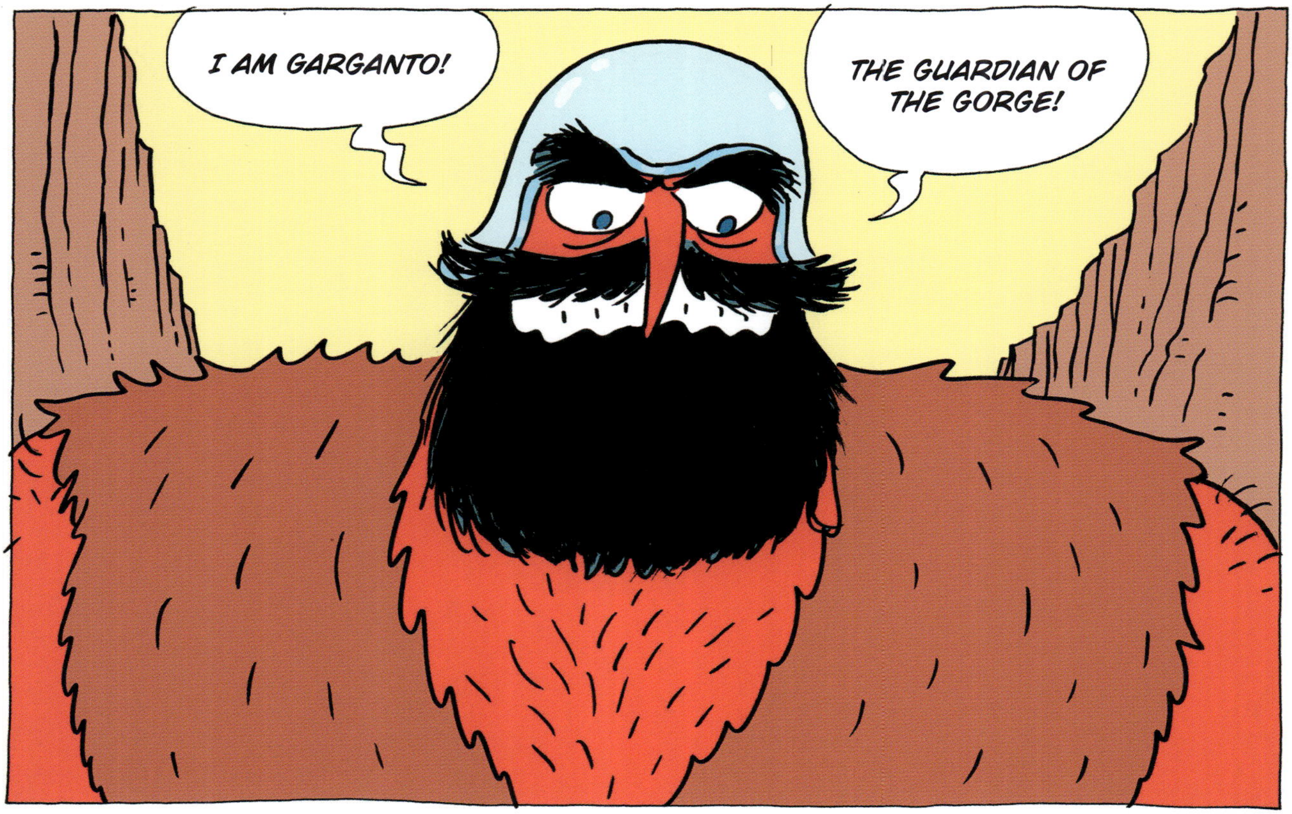
I AM GARGANTO!
THE GUARDIAN OF THE GORGE!

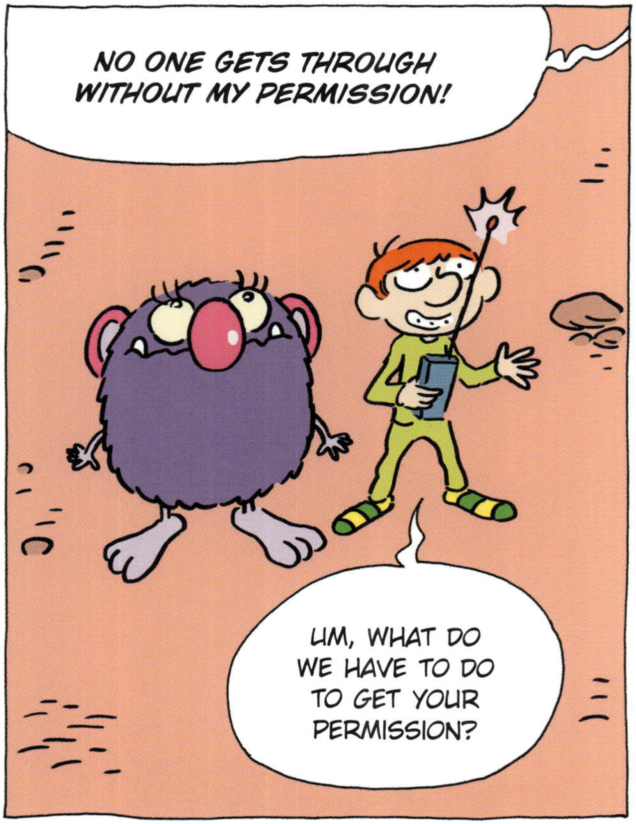
NO ONE GETS THROUGH WITHOUT MY PERMISSION!
UM, WHAT DO WE HAVE TO DO TO GET YOUR PERMISSION?

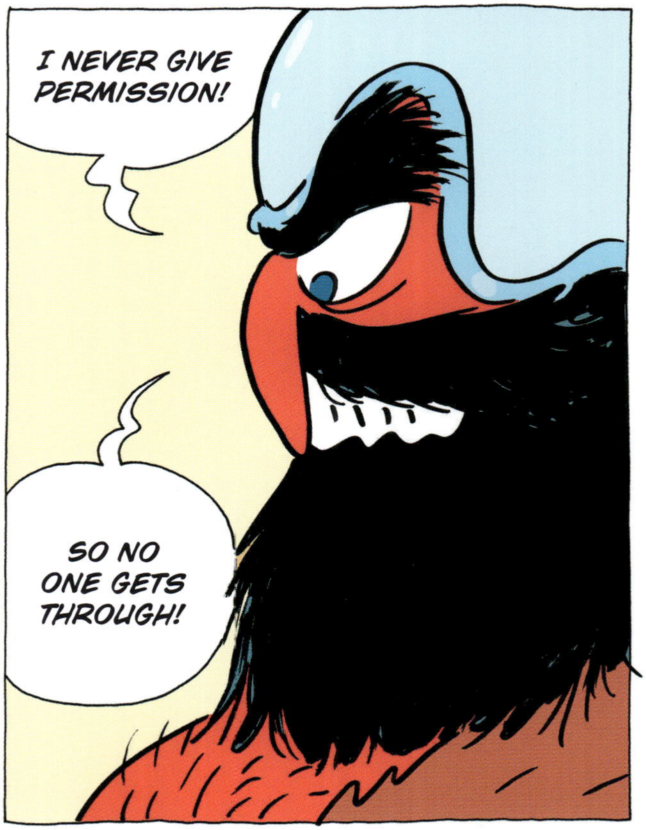
I NEVER GIVE PERMISSION!
SO NO ONE GETS THROUGH!

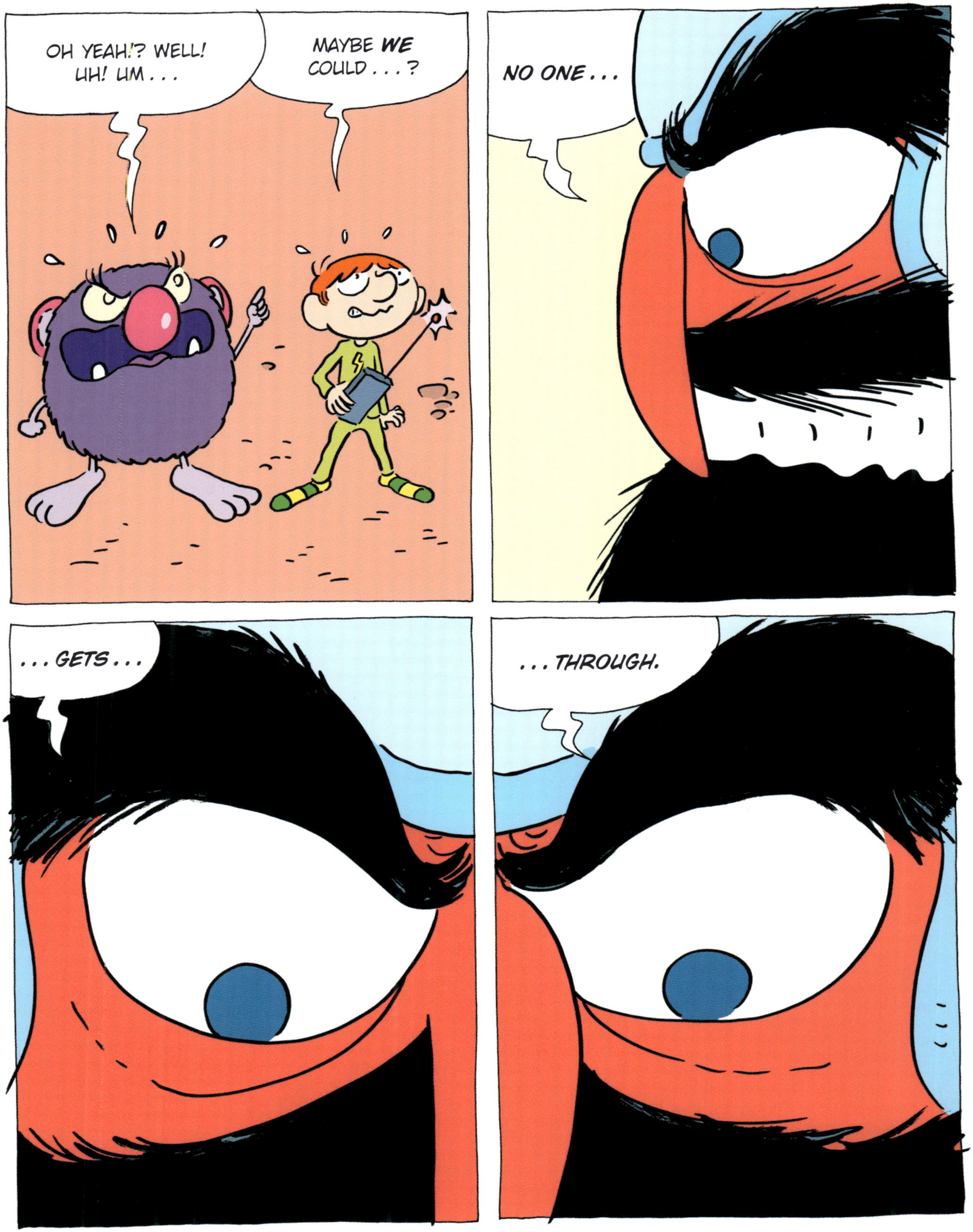
OH YEAH!? WELL! UH! UM . . .
MAYBE WE COULD . . . ?
NO ONE . . .
. . . GETS . . .
. . . THROUGH.

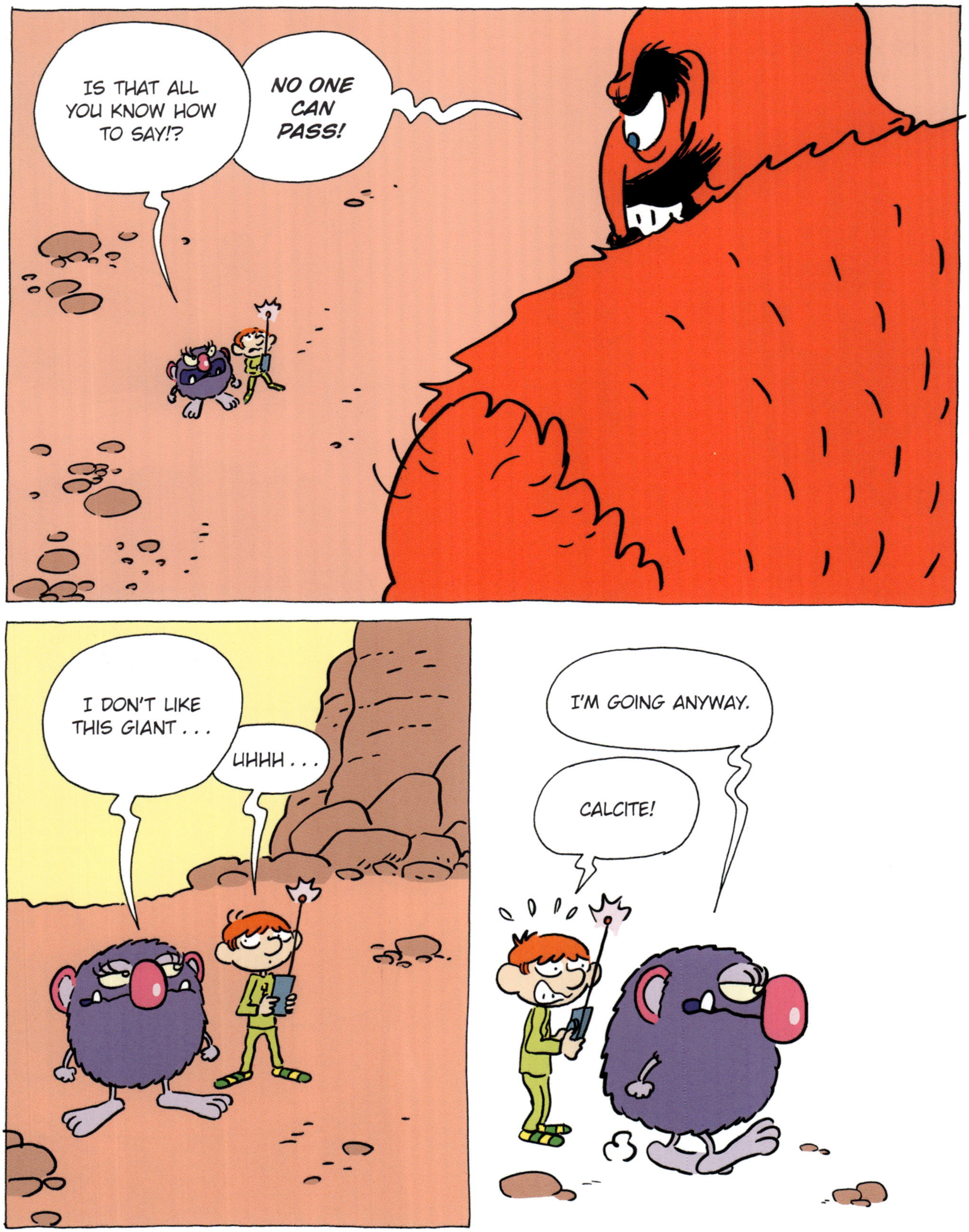
IS THAT ALL YOU KNOW HOW TO SAY!?
NO ONE CAN PASS!
I DON'T LIKE THIS GIANT . . .
UHHH . . .
I'M GOING ANYWAY.
CALCITE!

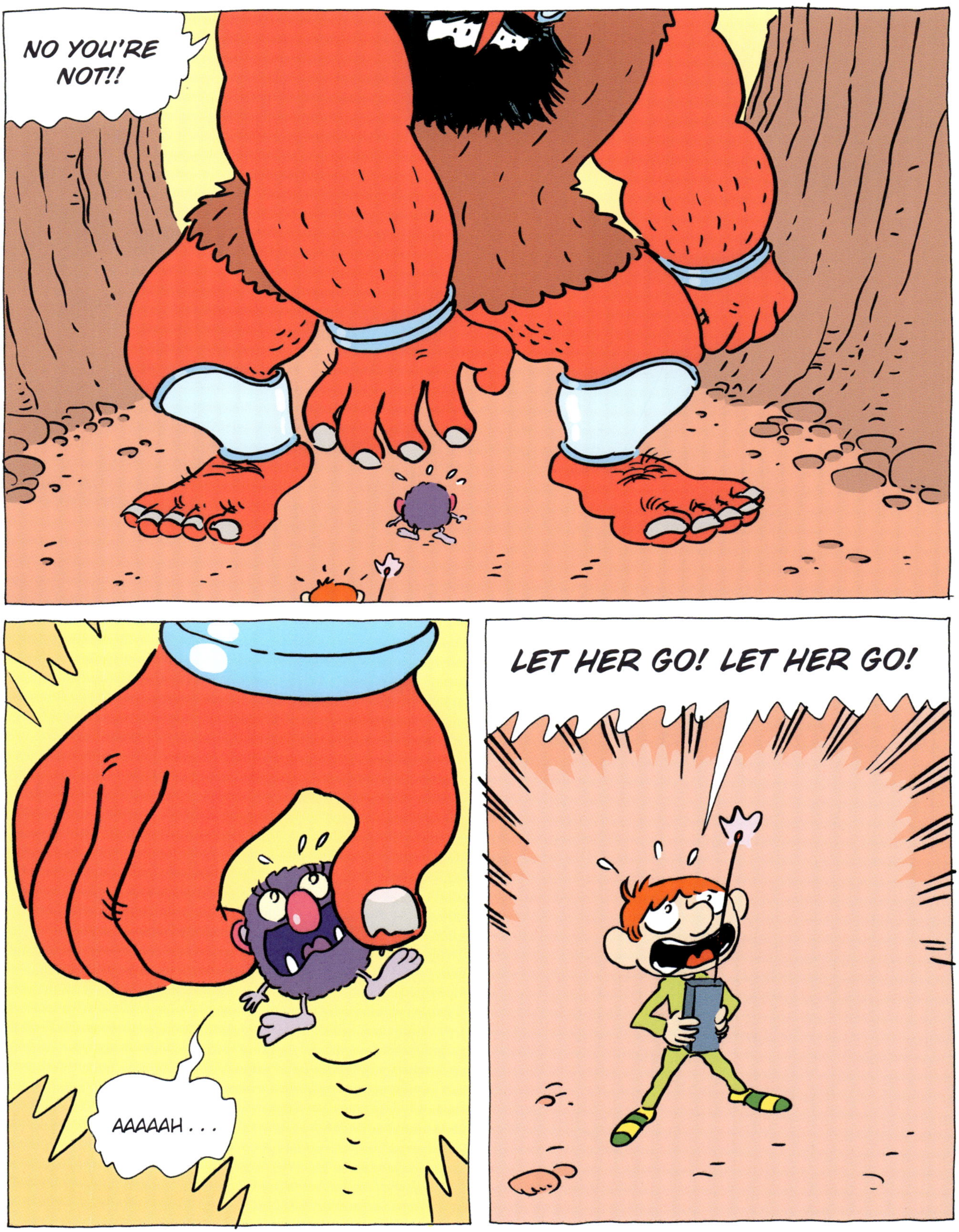
NO YOU'RE NOT!!
AAAAAH . . .
LET HER GO! LET HER GO!

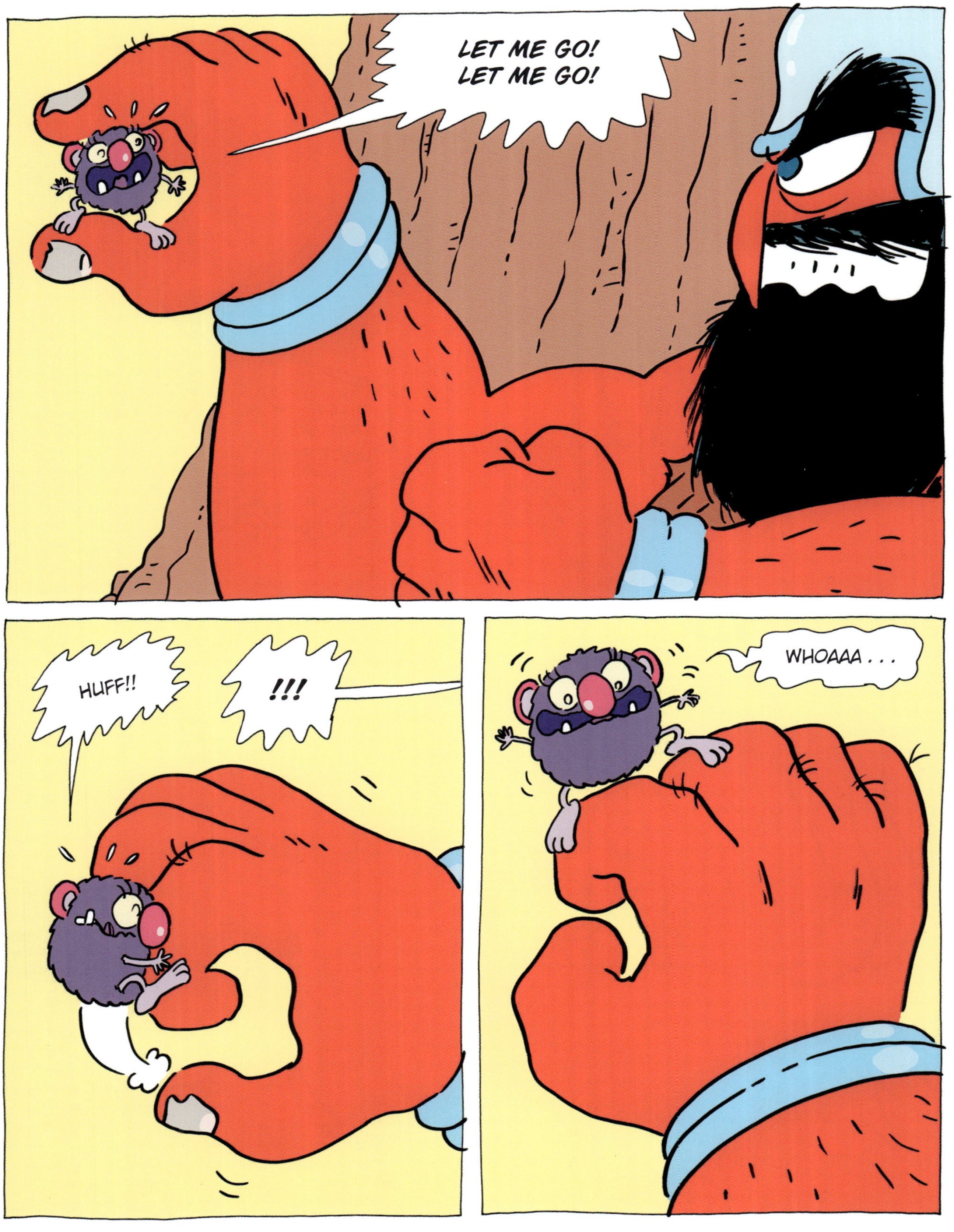
LET ME GO!
LET ME GO!
HUFF!!
!!!
WHOAAA . . .

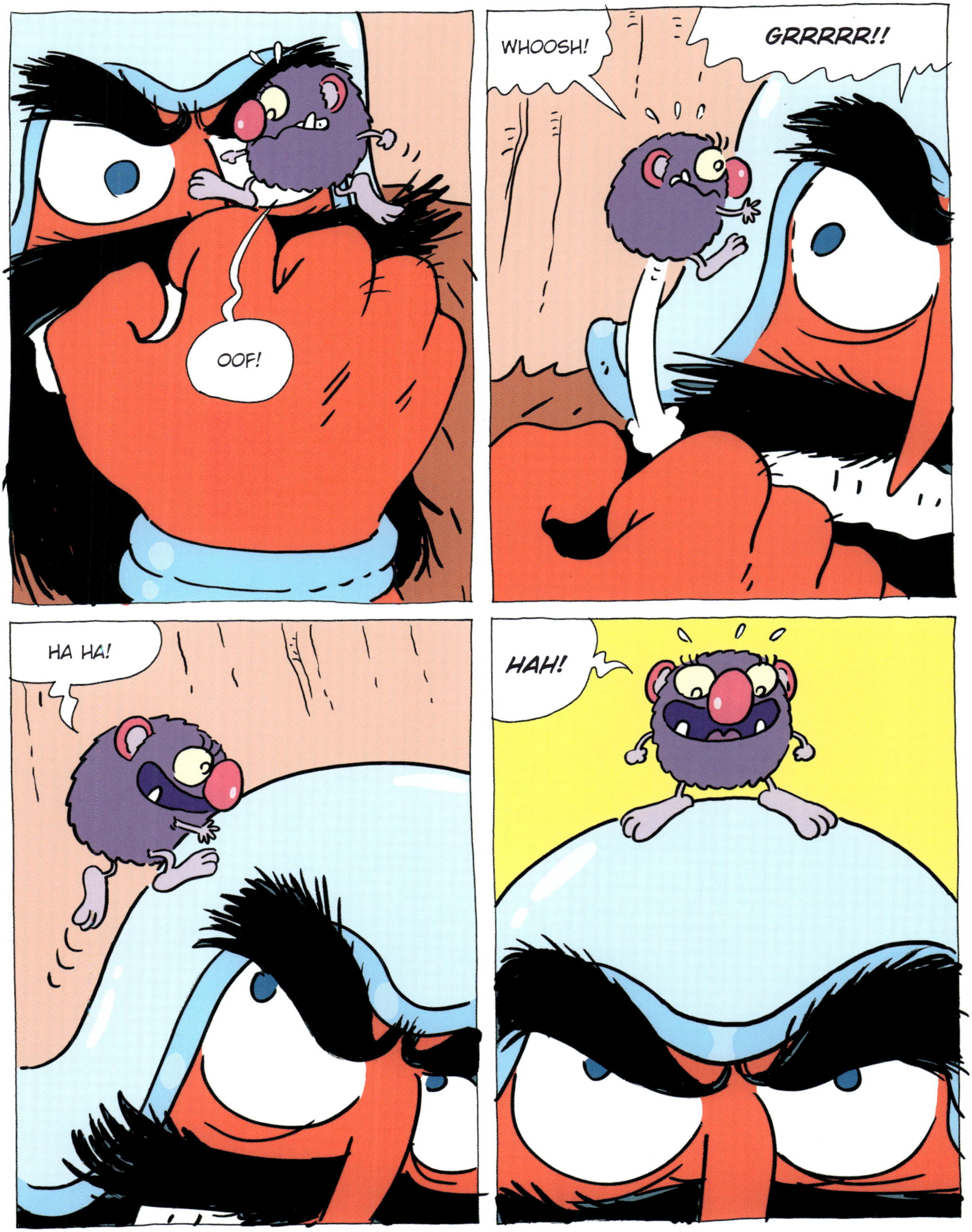
OOF!
WHOOSH!
GRRRRR!!
HA HA!
HAH!

Panel 1:
RRR!!
NO ONE CAN PASS?

Panel 2:
YOU SURE?

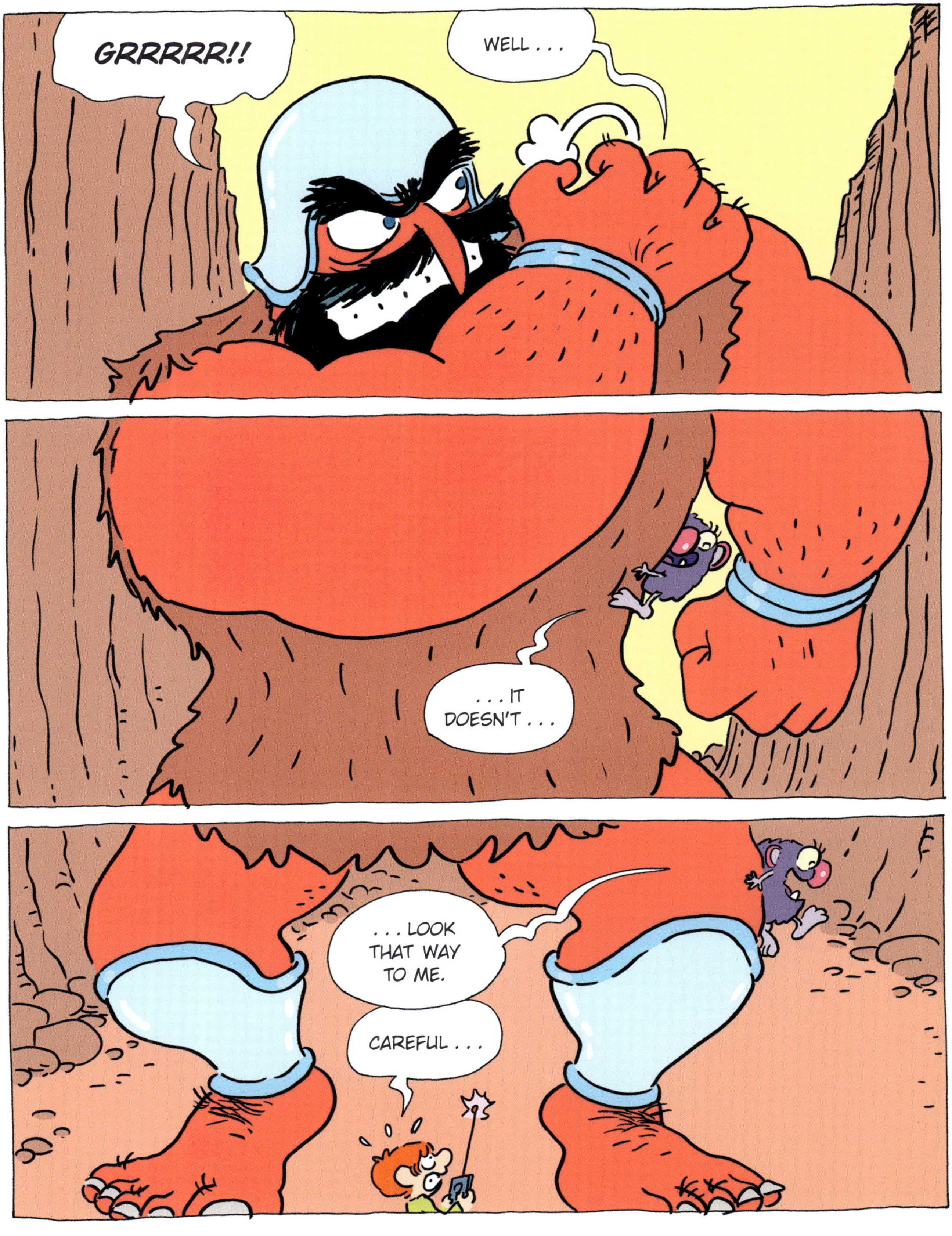
GRRRRR!!
WELL . . .
. . . IT DOESN'T . . .
. . . LOOK THAT WAY TO ME.
CAREFUL . . .

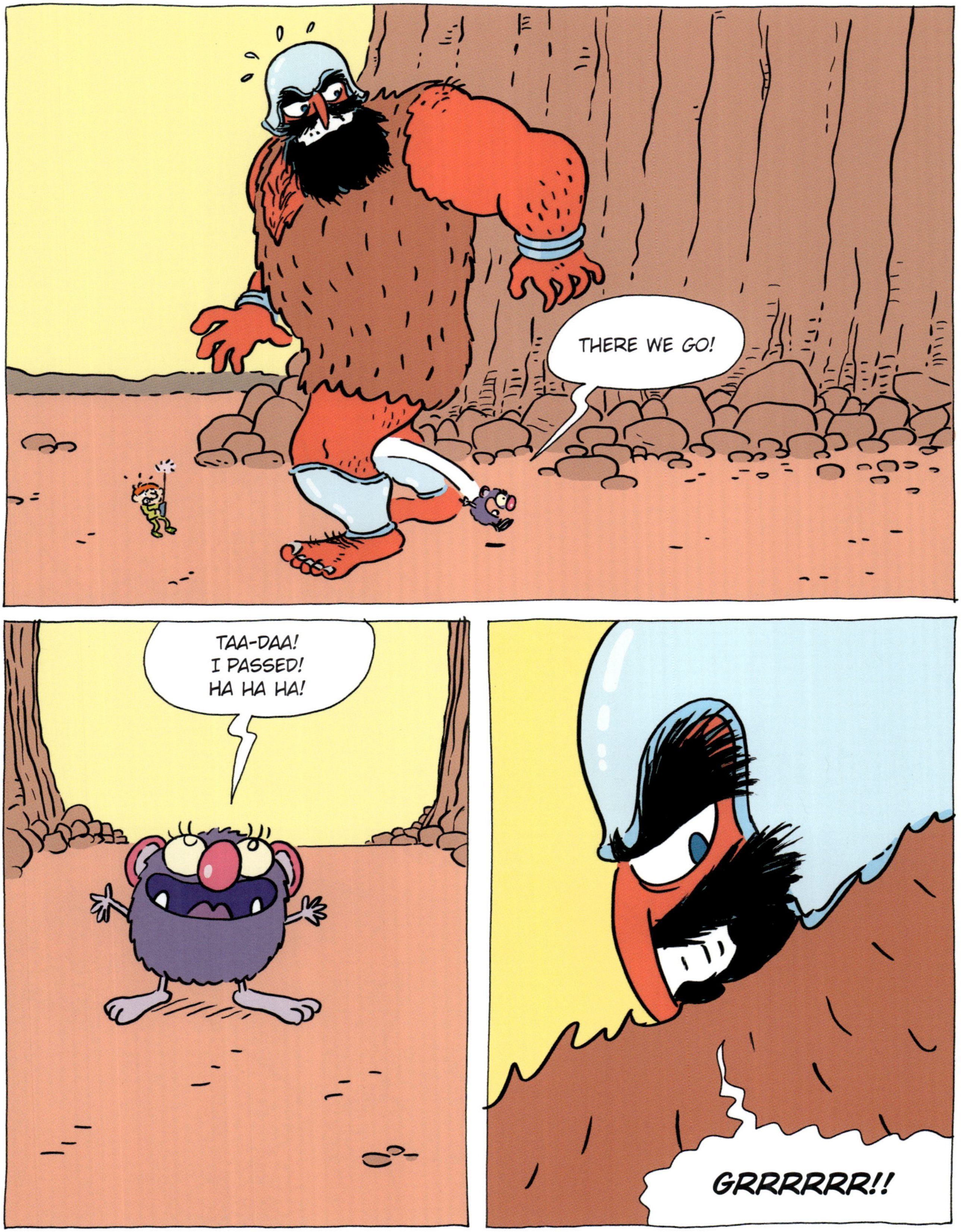
THERE WE GO!
TAA-DAA! I PASSED! HA HA HA!
GRRRRRR!!

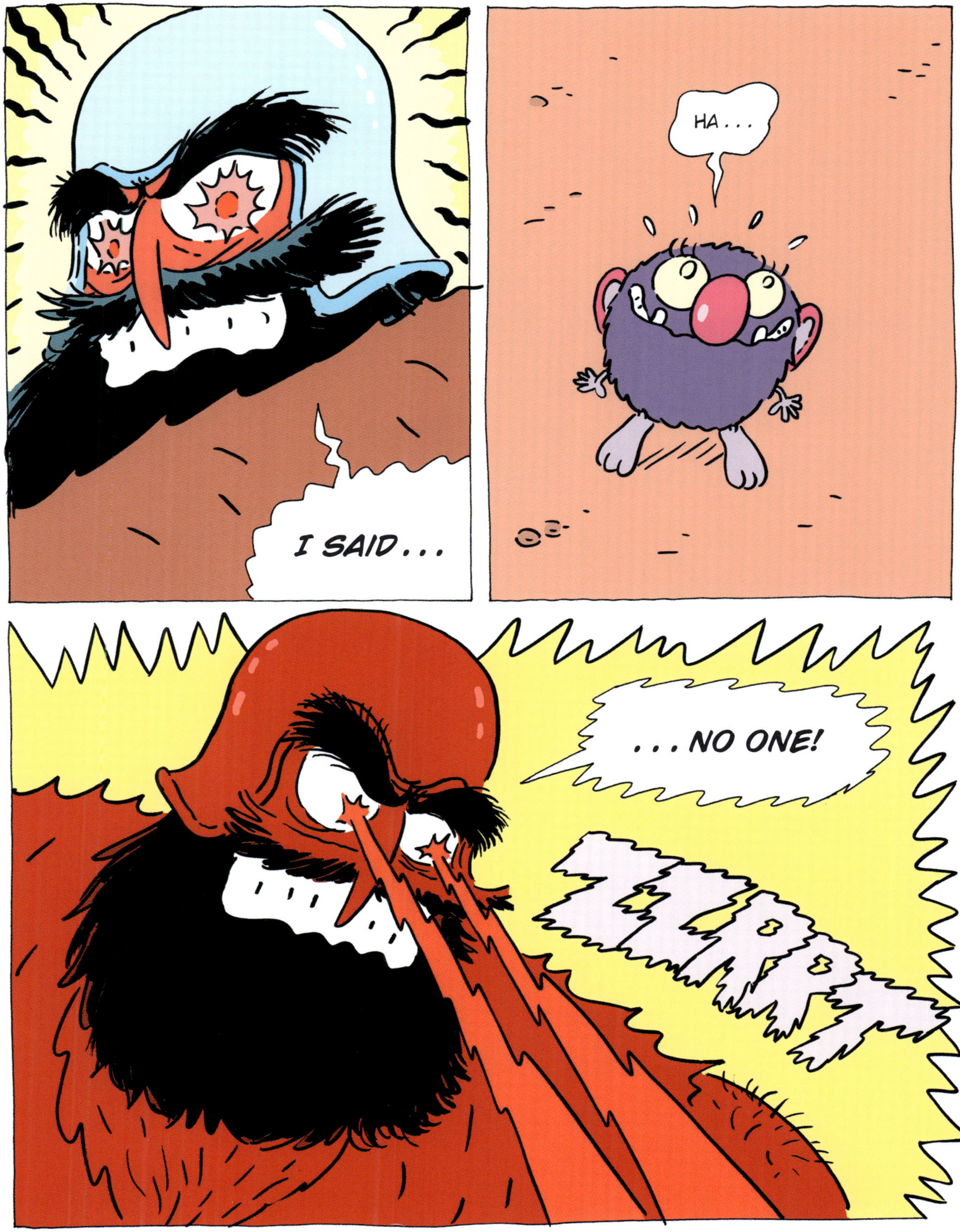
I SAID . . .
HA . . .
. . . NO ONE!
ZZRRT

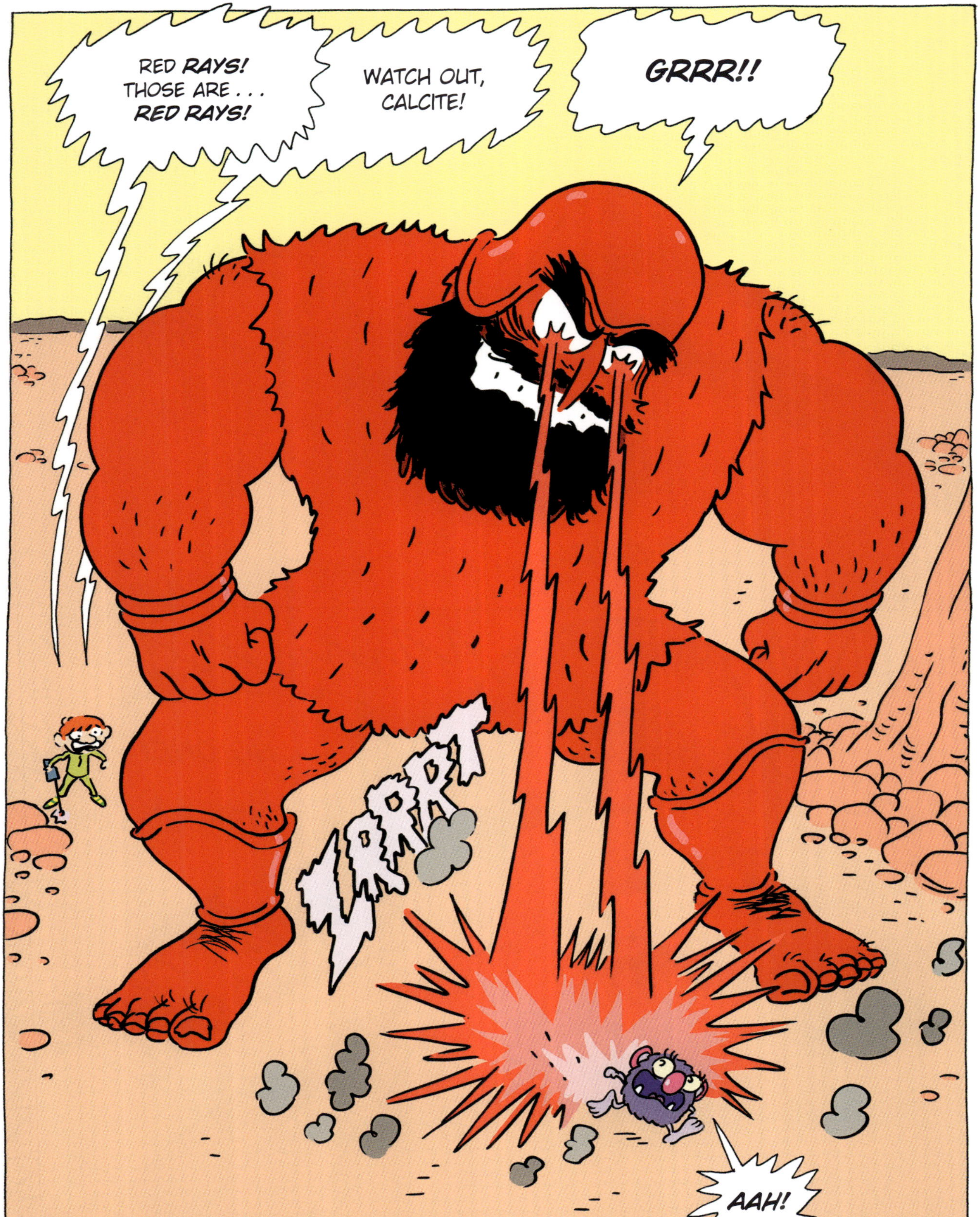
RED RAYS! THOSE ARE . . . RED RAYS!
WATCH OUT, CALCITE!
GRRR!!
ZRRRT
AAH!

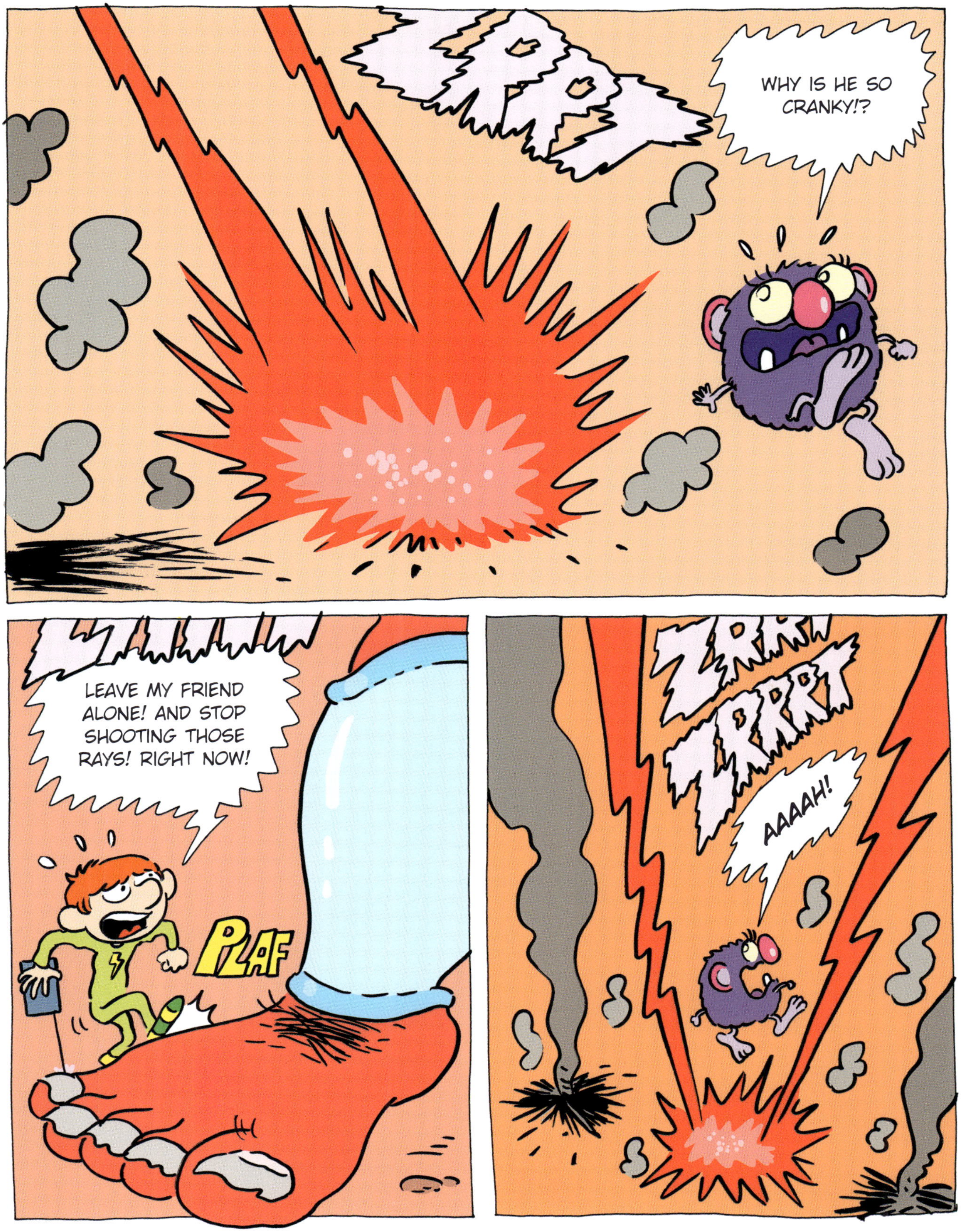
ZRRT
WHY IS HE SO CRANKY!?
LEAVE MY FRIEND ALONE! AND STOP SHOOTING THOSE RAYS! RIGHT NOW!
PLAF
ZRRRT
AAAAH!

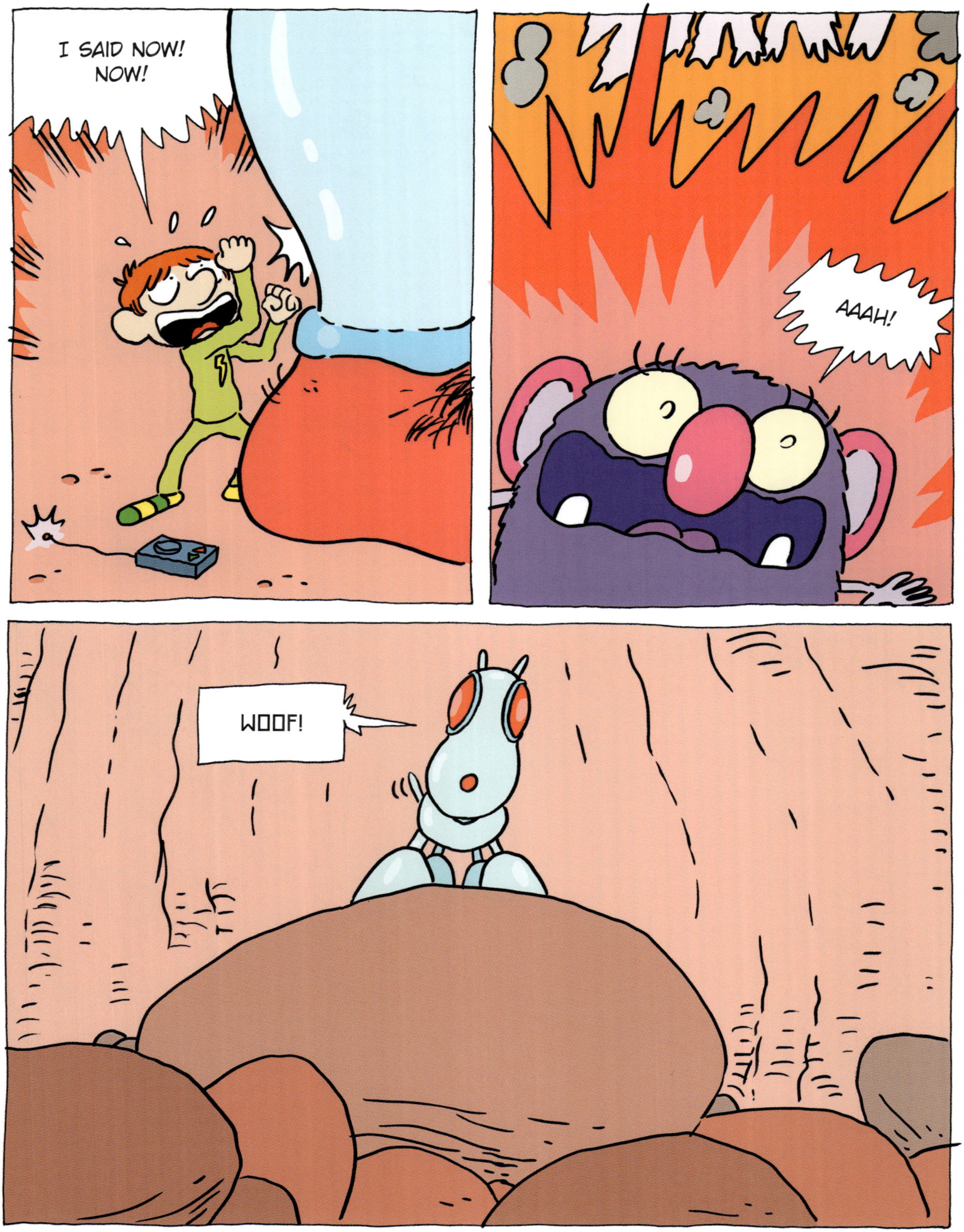
I SAID NOW! NOW!
AAAH!
WOOF!

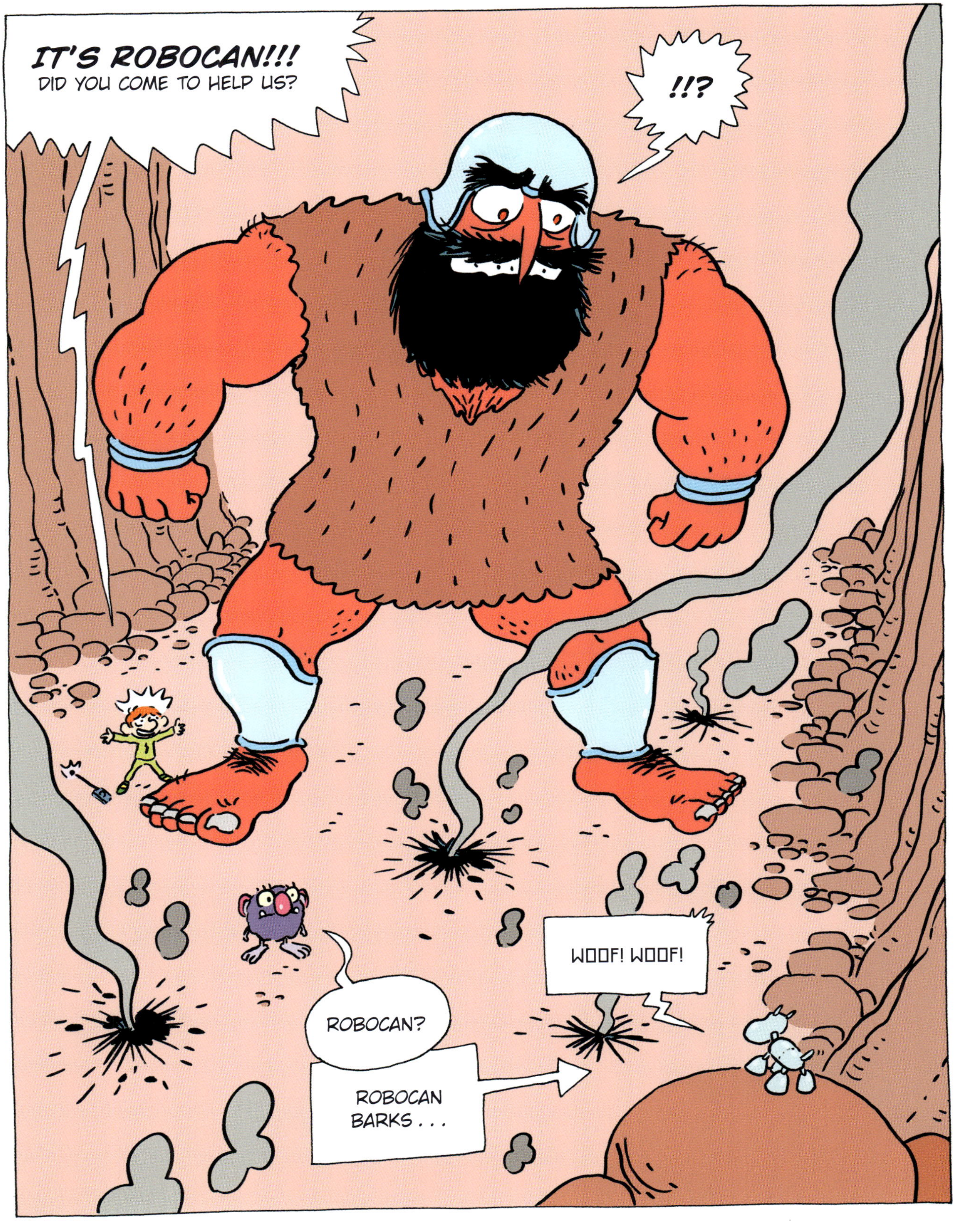
IT'S ROBOCAN!!!
DID YOU COME TO HELP US?
!!?
ROBOCAN?
WOOF! WOOF!
ROBOCAN BARKS . . .

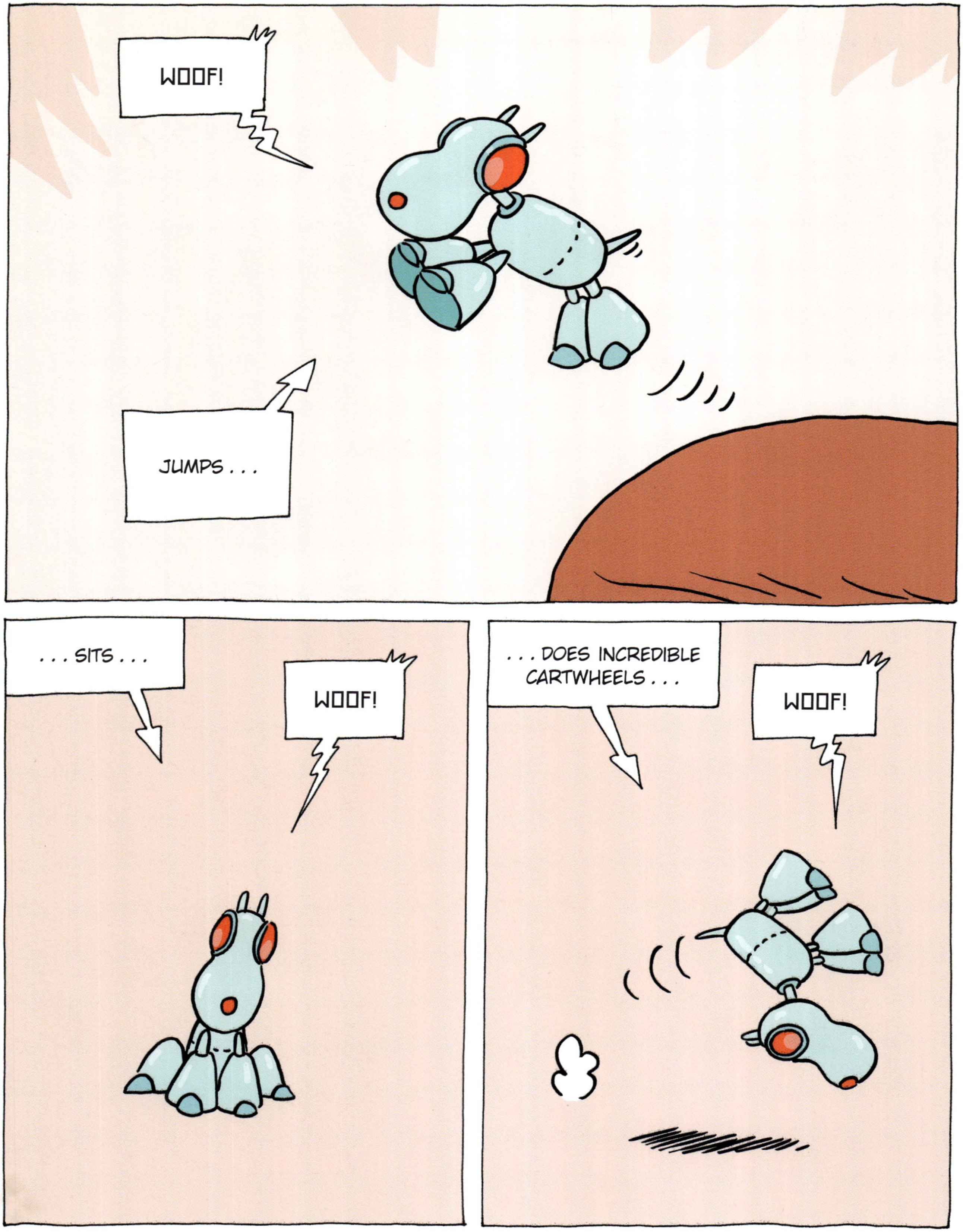
WOOF!
JUMPS . . .
. . . SITS . . .
WOOF!
. . . DOES INCREDIBLE CARTWHEELS . . .
WOOF!

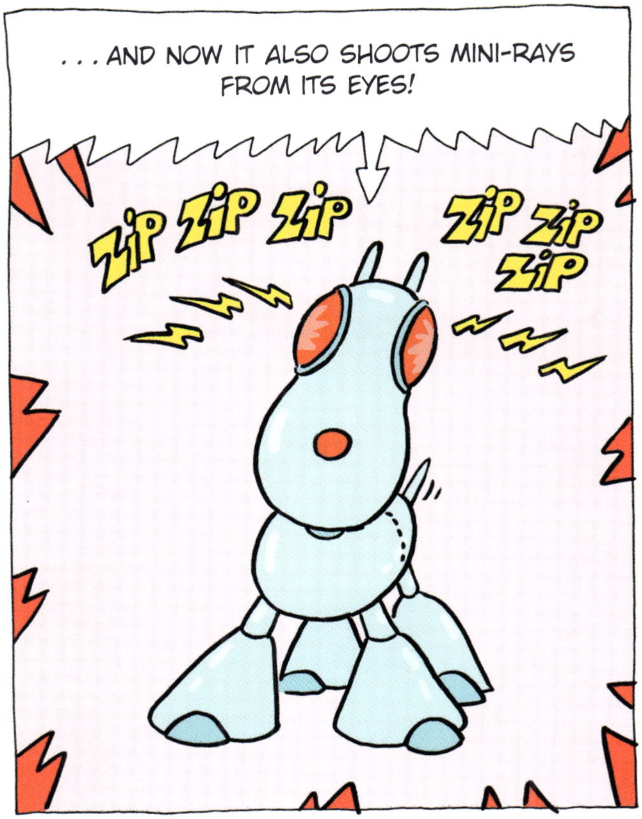
. . . AND NOW IT ALSO SHOOTS MINI-RAYS FROM ITS EYES!
ZIP ZIP ZIP
ZIP ZIP ZIP

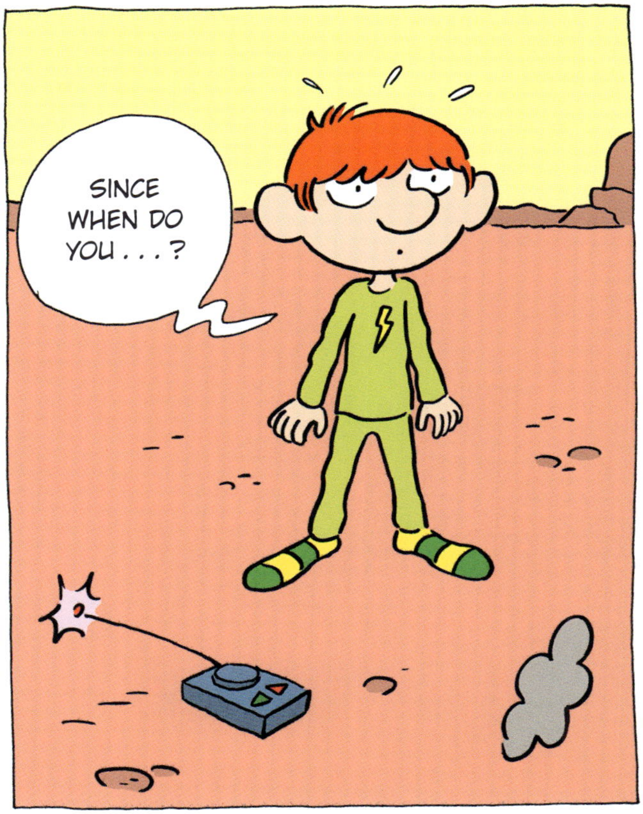
SINCE WHEN DO YOU . . . ?

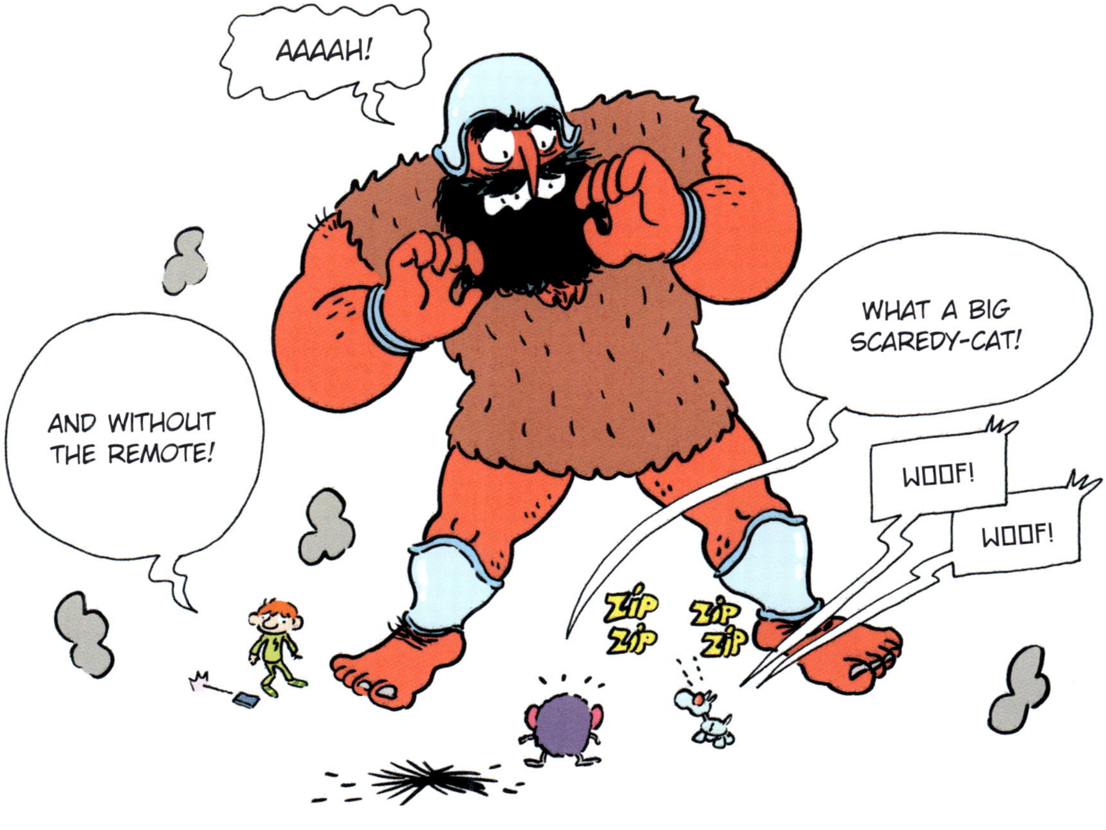
AAAAH!
WHAT A BIG SCAREDY-CAT!
AND WITHOUT THE REMOTE!
WOOF!
WOOF!
ZIP ZIP
ZIP ZIP

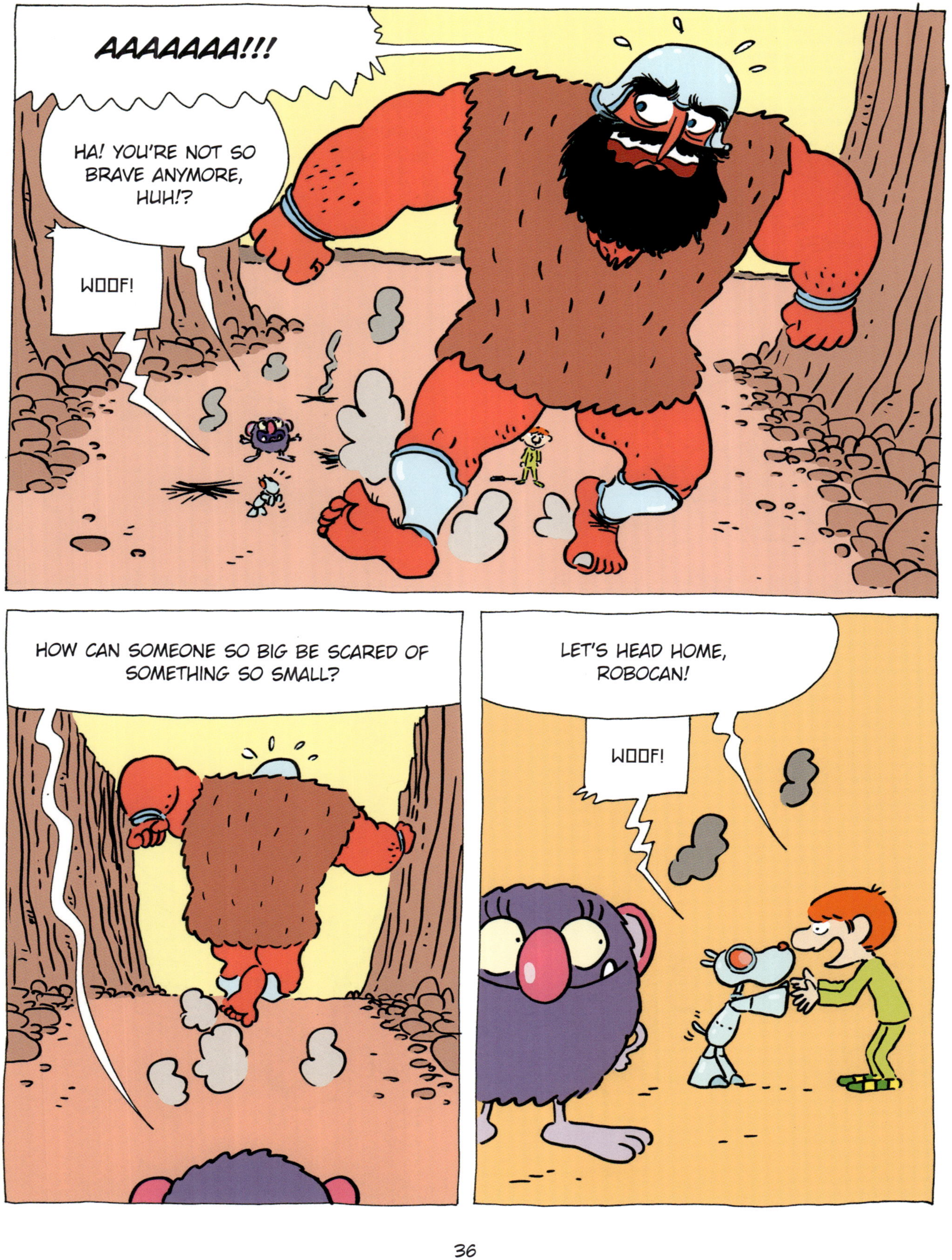
AAAAAAA!!!
HA! YOU'RE NOT SO BRAVE ANYMORE, HUH!?
WOOF!
HOW CAN SOMEONE SO BIG BE SCARED OF SOMETHING SO SMALL?
LET'S HEAD HOME, ROBOCAN!
WOOF!

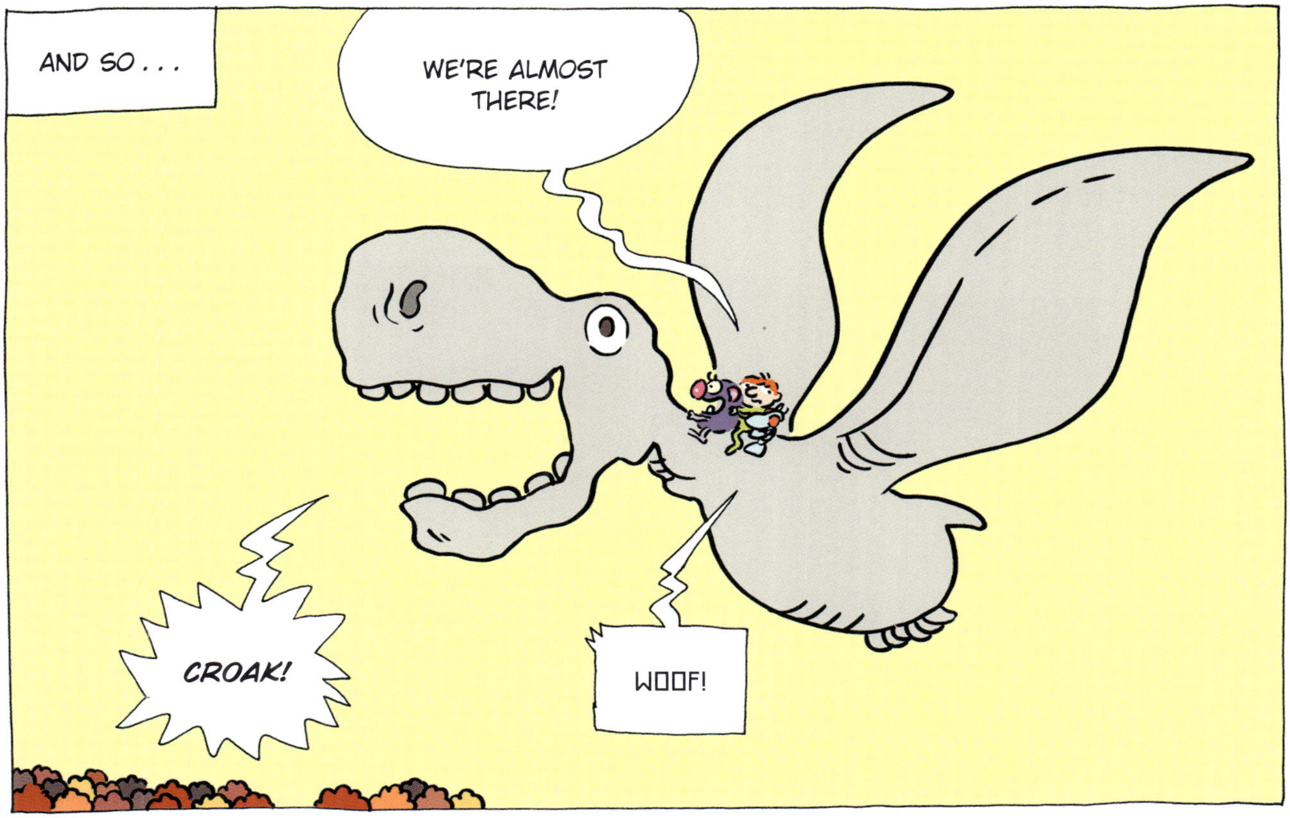
AND SO . . .
WE'RE ALMOST THERE!
CROAK!
WOOF!

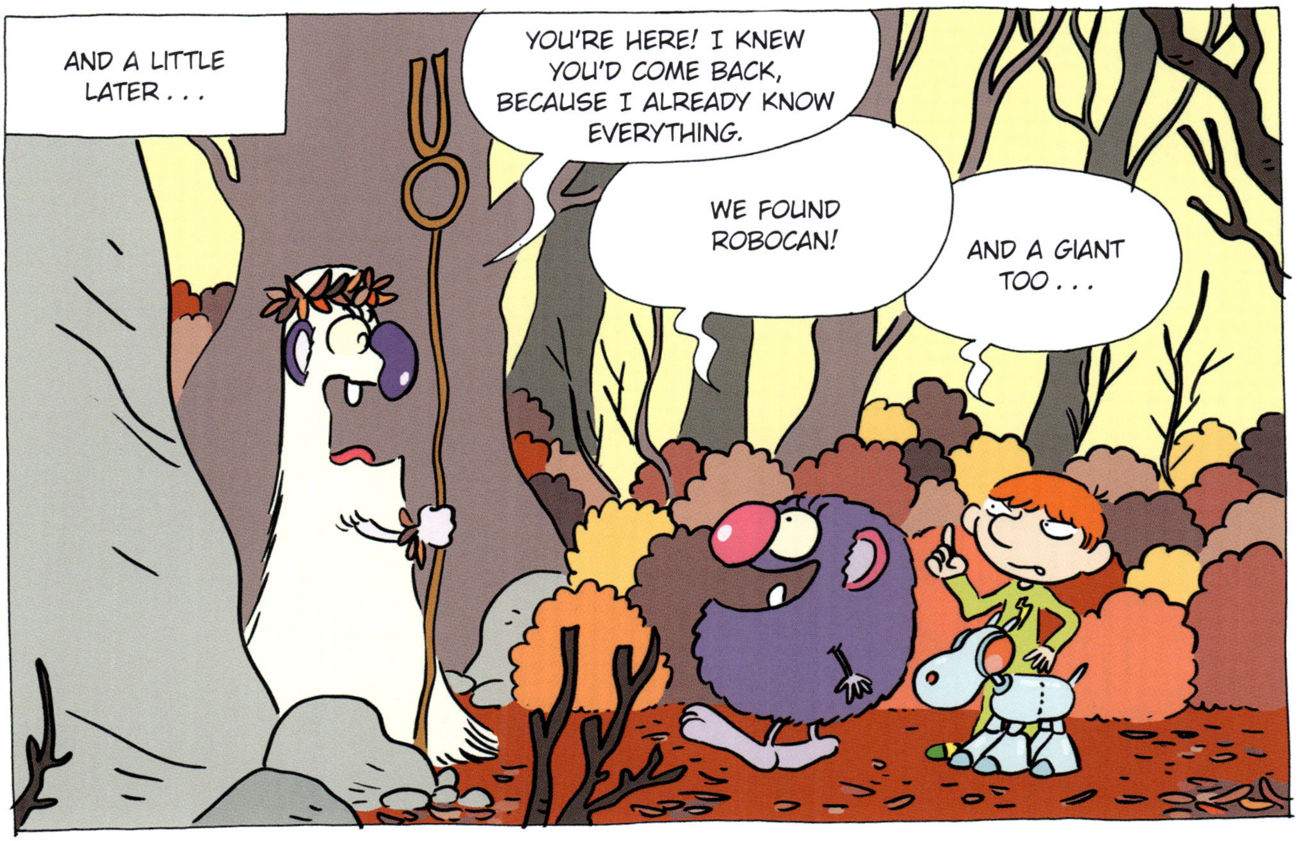
AND A LITTLE LATER . . .
YOU'RE HERE! I KNEW YOU'D COME BACK, BECAUSE I ALREADY KNOW EVERYTHING.
WE FOUND ROBOCAN!
AND A GIANT TOO . . .

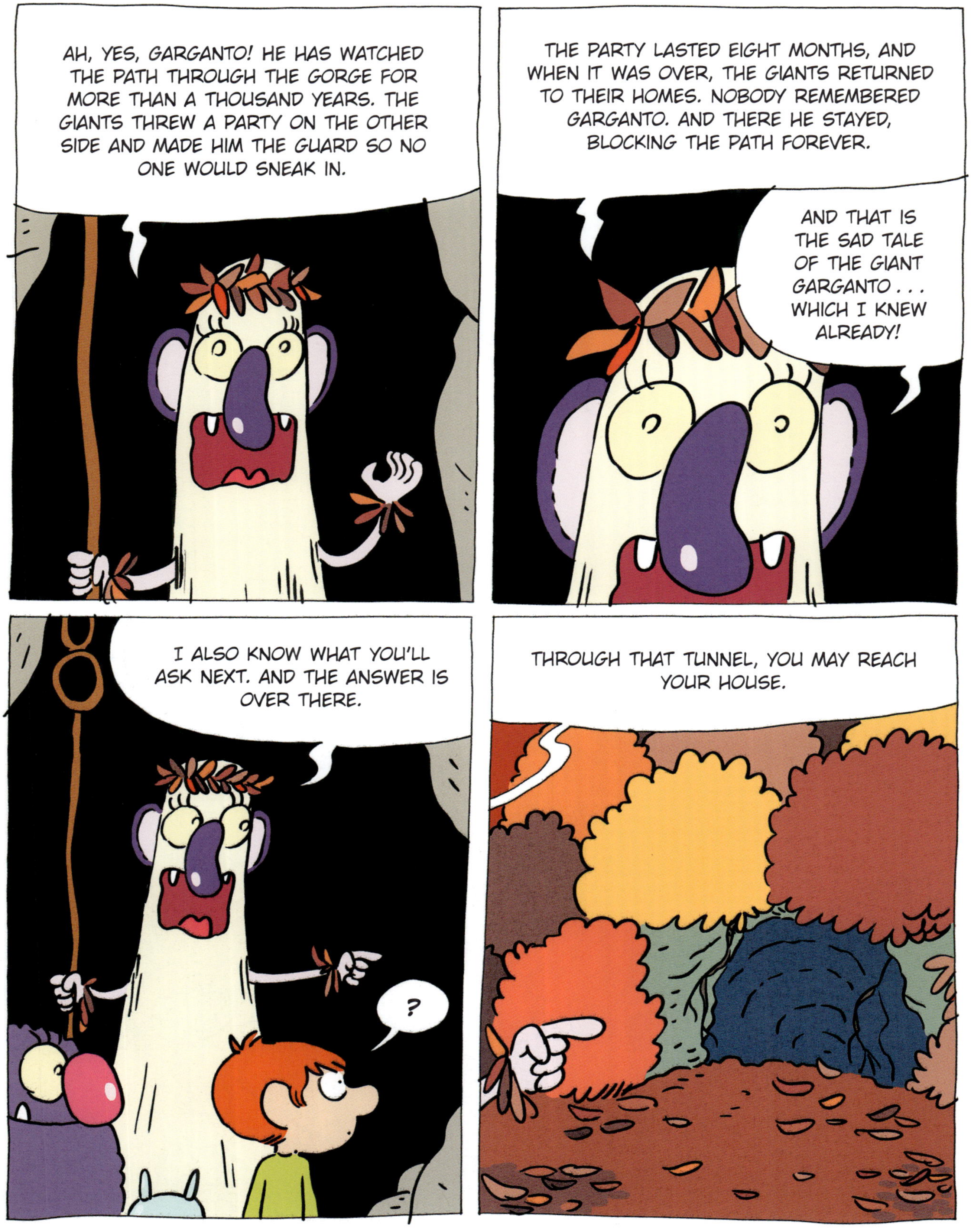

AH, YES, GARGANTO! HE HAS WATCHED THE PATH THROUGH THE GORGE FOR MORE THAN A THOUSAND YEARS. THE GIANTS THREW A PARTY ON THE OTHER SIDE AND MADE HIM THE GUARD SO NO ONE WOULD SNEAK IN.
THE PARTY LASTED EIGHT MONTHS, AND WHEN IT WAS OVER, THE GIANTS RETURNED TO THEIR HOMES. NOBODY REMEMBERED GARGANTO. AND THERE HE STAYED, BLOCKING THE PATH FOREVER.
AND THAT IS THE SAD TALE OF THE GIANT GARGANTO . . . WHICH I KNEW ALREADY!
I ALSO KNOW WHAT YOU'LL ASK NEXT. AND THE ANSWER IS OVER THERE.
?
THROUGH THAT TUNNEL, YOU MAY REACH YOUR HOUSE.

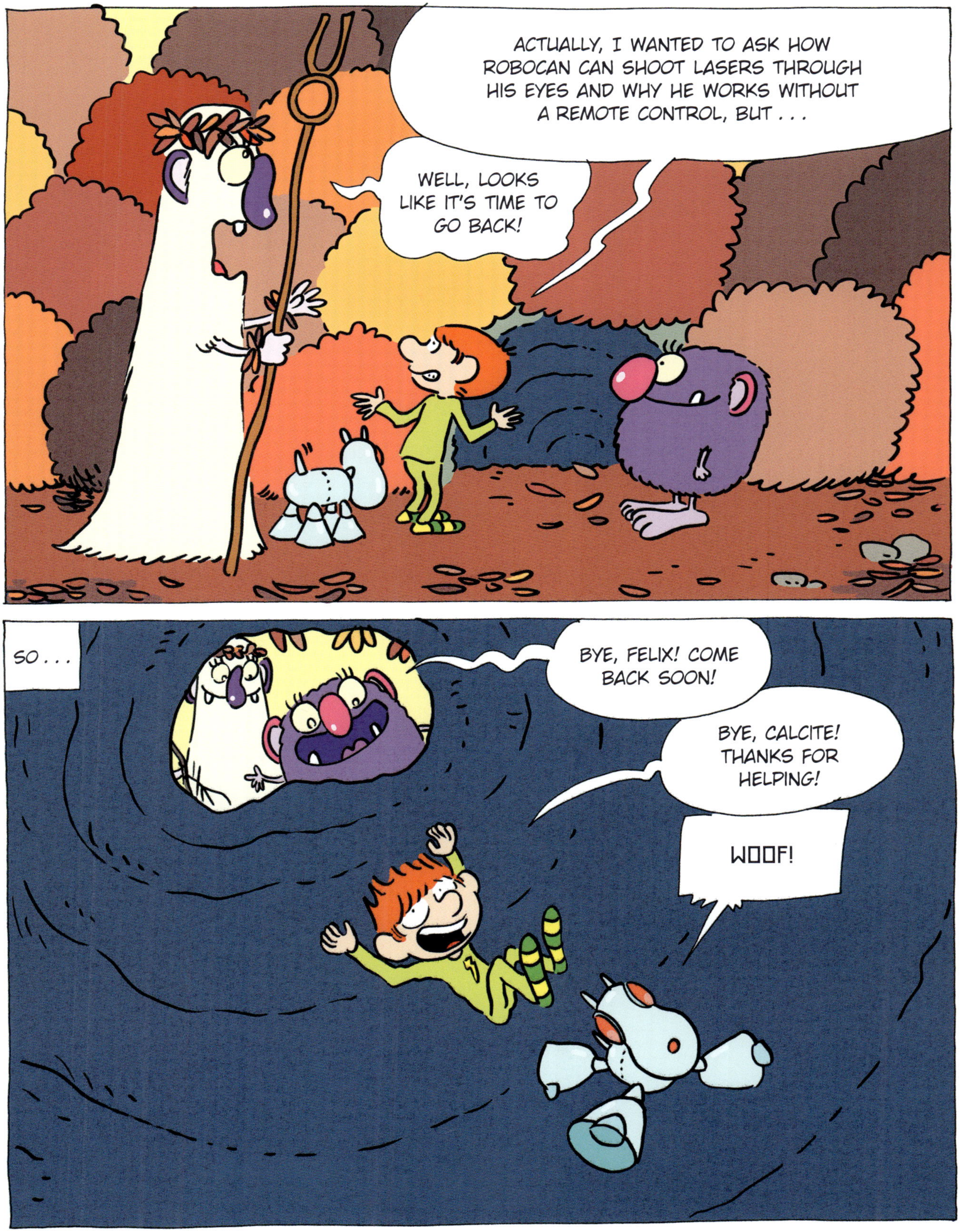
ACTUALLY, I WANTED TO ASK HOW ROBOCAN CAN SHOOT LASERS THROUGH HIS EYES AND WHY HE WORKS WITHOUT A REMOTE CONTROL, BUT . . .
WELL, LOOKS LIKE IT'S TIME TO GO BACK!
SO . . .
BYE, FELIX! COME BACK SOON!
BYE, CALCITE! THANKS FOR HELPING!
WOOF!

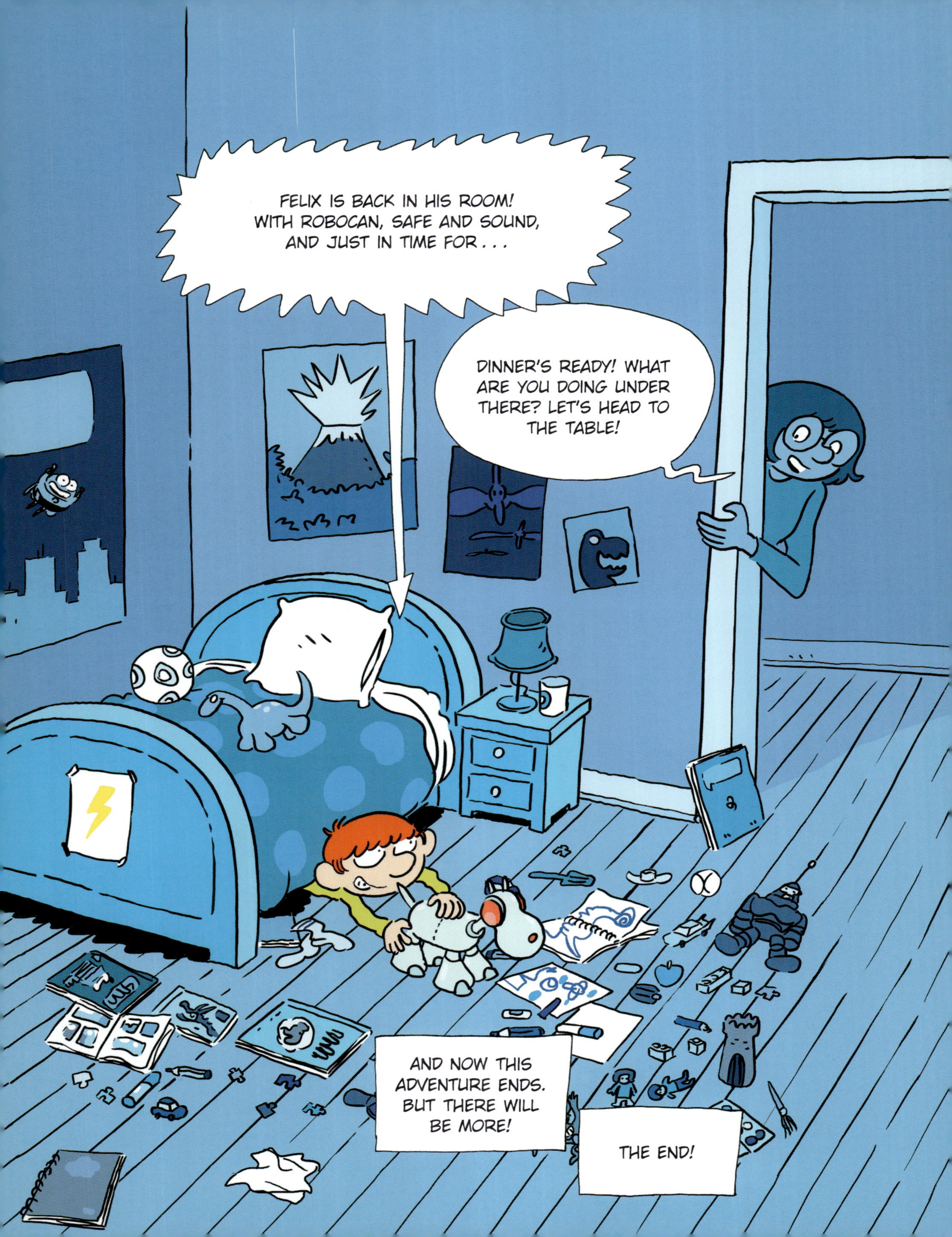
FELIX IS BACK IN HIS ROOM! WITH ROBOCAN, SAFE AND SOUND, AND JUST IN TIME FOR . . .
DINNER'S READY! WHAT ARE YOU DOING UNDER THERE? LET'S HEAD TO THE TABLE!
AND NOW THIS ADVENTURE ENDS. BUT THERE WILL BE MORE!
THE END!

ROBOCAN HAS SCARED THE GIANT. BUT THIS GIANT IS ALSO AFRAID OF SPIDERS. FIND THE SPIDER HIDDEN SOMEWHERE IN THIS BOOK AND YOU CAN SCARE A GIANT OF YOUR OWN.

FELIX and CALCITE
#1 THE LAND OF THE TROLLS
Artur Laperla

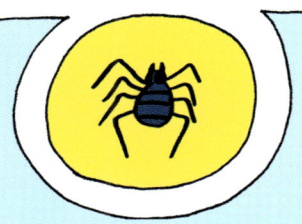

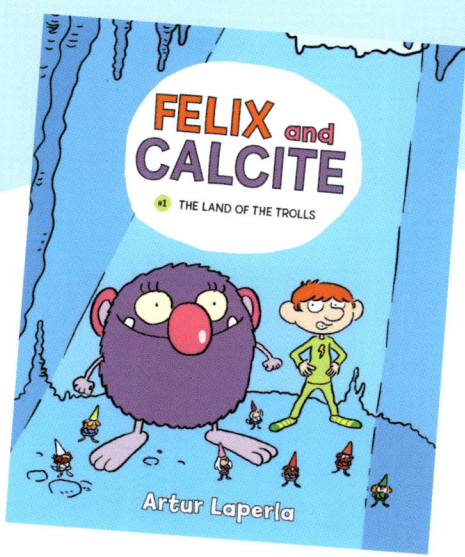

DON'T FORGET TO READ THE FIRST ADVENTURE OF

FELIX and CALCITE

THE LAND OF THE TROLLS

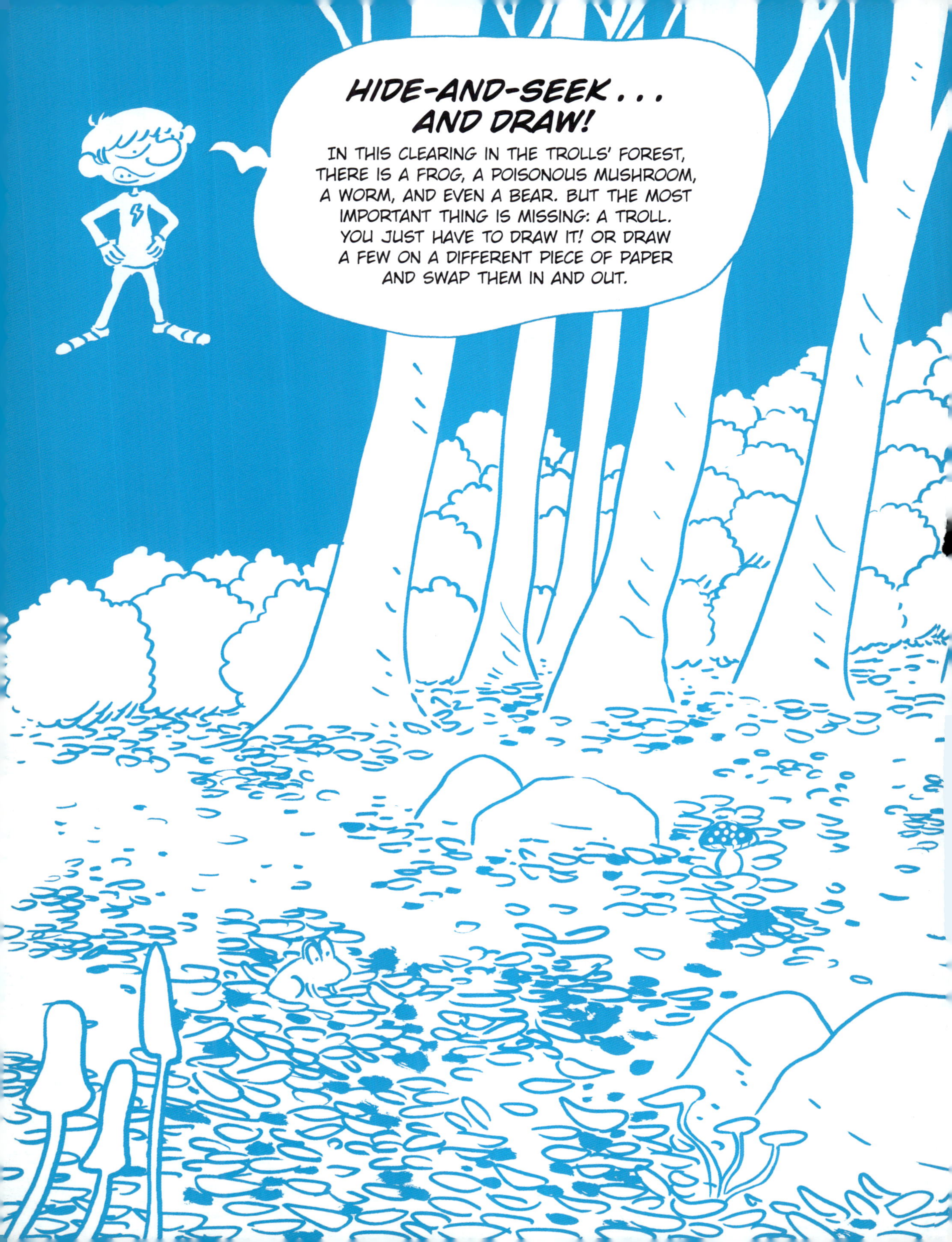
HIDE-AND-SEEK . . .
. . . AND DRAW!
IN THIS CLEARING IN THE TROLLS' FOREST, THERE IS A FROG, A POISONOUS MUSHROOM, A WORM, AND EVEN A BEAR. BUT THE MOST IMPORTANT THING IS MISSING: A TROLL. YOU JUST HAVE TO DRAW IT! OR DRAW A FEW ON A DIFFERENT PIECE OF PAPER AND SWAP THEM IN AND OUT.